Bombyonder

Bombyonder

Reb Livingston

Bitter Cherry Books
Atlanta, GA
2014

Copyright © 2014 by Reb Livingston
Published by Bitter Cherry Books
Distributed by Coconut, www.coconutpoetry.org
All rights reserved
ISBN: 978-0-9907582-0-4

Cover Design: Charlie Orr
Proofreaders: Joe Massey & Heather Weaver

This book is a work of fiction. All characters in this novel are fictitious. Any resemblance to actual events or locales or persons, living or dead, is entirely coincidental.

Bombyonder

Some kind of war happened at some time or another and continued for quite some time to come. There had to be an end to it, sometime, but when that time would be I couldn't say. What I could say was that historians from another time, along with the archivists, archaeologists and scuba divers from that same time discovered some kind of bomb, one of the kinds of bombs invented by my father, a bomb he slowly worked on for most of his existence to ensure he maintained an existence after he was long gone. Once this discovery was made, my life was never recorded the same.

My father referred to the bomb as his philanthropy, explained that most academics are known for such philanthropy yet haven't the time or inclination as they should to work on philanthropy because there are so many tests and papers to grade, so many conferences to attend, so many committees to chair, so many responsibilities just to exist in the present that kept them away from building and preserving their names. For when the time came to recall these existing-for-the-present academics they no longer existed. They squandered their existence because they didn't use it to pursue their philanthropy. Existence without philanthropy doesn't exist in the books.

"I'm not afraid of dying, dying is one of the necessary ingredients. I acknowledge the imprints in cement. But I am concerned with being written into abstraction. Nobody bothers with the abstract. If nobody remembers my name, I was never here and if I wasn't here, I never happened. We can't happen without others remembering and comprehending a simple narrative skeleton. It's a tricky job speaking for the dead. You can't leave it to the living. You must leave them a script," my father explained.

For years he tried to stave off the army of demanding human need, but there was a war that needed ending. Philanthropy, this kind of philanthropy, took time to establish. He needed more years, more of this kind . . . this kindness, because this was to be his legacy, the legacy of the KIND BOMB.

Until the time came when there was no more time to give to his day-to-day existence, not if he wanted to exist in the first place. The bomb was needed immediately. So my father took a sabbatical from his day-to-day existence and got to work on his philanthropy to meet the requirements for achieving a recognized existence. Ready or not, he invented his legacy.

This kind of bomb, with its many brightly lit wires, consisted of a variety of impressive colors and sheens positively twinkling. I could not help but want to touch it. When I did touch it, it felt small, potent, much unlike any man I ever encountered. The urge to swallow it whole overwhelmed me. A new experience. For until that point my life was a topical survey of all things underwhelming. Little impressed. Or excited. Or felt worth investigating.

I wanted to know all about this kind bomb and asked my father many questions.

When the bomb goes off will there be a flash? Will people and buildings explode or will they incinerate? Will people be able to breathe? Will their lungs, eyes and skin burn? Will they be able to see? Will future generations be born without heads? Will men's testicles have more or less hair? Will women still have to wax? Will gender reflect in the symptoms? When the bomb strikes will there be a loud boom? Will it damage people's hearing? Will it cause blindness? Will there be smoke? Radiation? Gas? Will the effects linger and if so, for how long? Is the bomb clean or dirty? How can a bomb be clean? What's the difference? Is there a kind of bomb that won't make such a mess?

Father was selective in his responses. He never cared for over-explanation. I could only glean that the bomb changed the enemy in some way and that was far more beneficial than killing them. He needed the enemy to continue existing so they could remember him, so their children would go to schools and cross bridges named after him. This was necessary because if he didn't live on after the fact, what was the point in living at all?

"Dead people don't write books or produce films or even tweet. The dead serve no purpose for me," he said and who could argue with that logic? Not that I would have even if I could. Father didn't care for me when I was disagreeable and I needed to be cared for, in some way, by someone.

Does the bomb target their emotions? Could we make the enemy love us? Make them stop desiring what we don't want them to desire and weren't going to let them have in the first place? A massacre of want? Of needs? What exactly are we annihilating?

My father wasn't specific, but aloof and silent, like my father. In those days I knew so little of my inherited gifts and precious curses. The gift was the curse and the curse was the gift. The gift arrived on a bomb and curse wrapped the gift in tinsel. After you swallow the gift it takes a while to digest, not everything easily makes its way through and what comes out can be a bit unsightly. That was the conundrum. What to do with all the unwanted, undumpable crap. It didn't go away on its own.

What if everyone in my neighborhood stood on our roofs and shot down planes, behaving like goddamn sky terrorists, instigating the army to drop this kind of bomb on top of us? What exactly would happen to us as we stood shooting our guns on our roofs?

A nearby soldier claimed that the bomb would have to fall directly on top of someone to kill him. He claimed to have seen it happen in battle to a good man who deserved better and god bless his soul. But my father claimed that even if the bomb directly hit a person, the event would not kill, only change him. Now this change might be that the person wished to die and if the following chain of events led to death, well that's another thing entirely and it would be unfair to pin such results on a perfectly kind bomb.

Father demonstrated by putting a bomb in a test dummy's mouth. The explosion was small and didn't leave a mark. It was all about smoke and invisibility, ripples and awe, shock and animals, cause and results freed from responsibility. That dummy's turds would be linked by tinsel, like paper doll cutouts. That dummy wasn't a dummy any longer. That dummy changed into something else entirely. Something worth mentioning.

What a nice bomb.

"Not nice, there's nothing NICE about this bomb or any bomb for that matter. This is a KIND bomb. There's a difference. Nice is how one behaves to contribute towards their outward appearance. People try to seem nice. Nice is a con. Being kind comes from within. Kindness has a humanity to it. There's no point in building a bomb if you don't account for what it does to humanity. The philanthropy becomes the legacy which is always about the humanity, the architecture, structure, the blueprints of society."

So what does the bomb do, Daddy? What does the bomb tear apart? What does the bomb change? What good is change without awareness or control, Daddy? What kind of kindness can a bomb bring?

Daddy?

Proposed Bomb Names Rejected By My Father

Tender Torpedo

Gentle Shell

Sympathetic Grenade

Mild Projectile

Rocket with a Heart of Gold

Whatchamacallit Dingbat

More About Bombs

Bombs are never about niceness, even when they're making you feel good, which is almost never the case. Bombs are about effect. Intended and unintended. The kindest bombs are the cruelest. Bombs are about theft of place. Bombs are rubble makers. Bombs are torn limbs, shrapnel, burns and skin grafts, shadows on cement. Bombs are loud and terrifying. Bombs go deep.

Ultimately bombs are the gift. The gift never asked, requested. The kind of gift only an assbeast would regift and wow if Christmas isn't all about the domino sequence of assbeasting. The gift is always the curse. While my father's reputation was based on his creation of the kind of bomb that destroyed your wanting, that wasn't his greatest philanthropy. Secretly, without the government's knowledge, he worked on a second bomb, a different kind of bomb in his own vision, of his own flesh, his true legacy bomb, a bomb in pharmaceutical form. A bomb to make you remember what didn't happen in ways that couldn't have been, but is absolutely, positively 100% true.

A bomb of delusions? Lies?

Not lies. Records. Discovery. Resurrection. Interpretation of data and its infinite reinterpretations. Repeat as necessary. Reconstruction. Revision. Replacement. Father explained that previous events aren't nearly as true as we think and events that never happened are equally true. Sometimes more true than the truth. Maybe we could retroactively change the past with our intentions? Pondering anything long enough could mean the possibility that it all really happened—every version, every conflicting fact realized and verified. Remembering what didn't happen is to remember what was forgotten and we need the awareness of what slipped away in the first bombing because what slips away never leaves. What slips away becomes particles in the air, sinks into the water, soil, the plants. It's in our food attaching itself to our thighs, stomachs and chests like shrapnel. We carry it all inside beneath our skin, deep in our hearts and livers. Sometimes, a part returns as an illness, via coughing and wheezing. When we feel it coming up, when we actually see it, we're shocked it was ever inside us. More shocking than phlegm, shit, cum, bright yellow discharge or even tiny human beings. The unrecognizable within and not knowing how or what. So we call a doctor for an interpretation that we can digest. We rename it as a medical condition. The names of illnesses are all reconstructions of what we cannot understand. Maybe we're already retroactively changing what happened to us. Maybe that diarrhea used to be a lung tumor. Maybe our life histories are built entirely on medical revisionism, constantly in flux.

This sounds new age, Daddy. You're a scientist, not a bullshit guru. This is just some shit you ponder while getting high with your colleagues. You're starting to sound demented.

I started becoming disagreeable.

"I'm whatever sounds most impressive at the time of impressing. Don't be so feeble-minded. Labels are deceptions to impress designed to distract."

Deception as a confusion tactic?

"Darling, that is the tactic of politics, bombs are never political, they simply annihilate," said the professor with his ties to the government, who was my father, an expert in the kind extermination that allowed certain names to live past their deaths, in an array of historical snippets. My father, bestower of the kindest bomb of all, would revolutionize existence. A bomb-induced existence allowing you to live while recreating memories. It got me thinking of possibilities for the future. A future where I existed not needing to be cared for. Or I existed completely cared for, under my own terms and desires.

Daddy, are you a weapon? What if I pushed you off a cliff, would you explode when you hit the ground? What if I already pushed you off that cliff? What if I smothered you with a pillow while you slept, would you stop breathing? What if I already smothered you with a pillow? Do you need to breathe to live? Are you even alive? Were you ever alive? Are you in the same realm as Dick Cheney? If you had a heart attack and your heart stopped, would you still function? Would a stroke stop your mind? Slow it down? Is there a weapon that could end a father's legacy? A weapon to fight the weapon? A weapon to stop the remembering? A gun or blade or body of water? Is there a bomb that would be effective against your philanthropy?

"You are a very silly girl. As if there would be anything at all for you, if it weren't for my philanthropy. My existence makes your existence possible."

This was another point I felt disagreeable about. Father perceived that he was the source of everything and what I was or could be was based on my relation to him. Like he was the Sun and I, the recently downgraded Pluto. Whereas I perceived him as a talking, heaving flail wrapped and bow-tied around my neck.

Of course it's natural for a daughter to have different beliefs than her father. Some of the most threatening things in life are completely natural.

Deep down my father believed that the most profound experience is the experiment of one's own children. Not the conception or the birth or the raising, but the bombing of his own creation to put in motion a profound action. Profound enough to be his mark. A professor's child, young or grown, is always the first to swallow the father's words, the hard pill, this fatherly bomb spreading, instructing bloodlines of the historical truth, the definitive ancestry. Such as the institution of family could not exist without its foundation of necessary neglect and brutality to carry on. This foundation matures or, depending on your perspective, festers with time. We don't "break away" or heal as we grow into adulthood, we become more entrenched in our ancestry. We become the marks we were created to symbolize.

Or the more accurate perversion of the intended mark.

At this point I was so grown I feared I began to shrink.

Father as weapon, mother as the seeded scorched Earth, buried offspring that grows into the leaking tree grown for arrows. The future imagined as projectiles, targets and comeuppance. Things were simpler in the past. Clearer, more concrete. My father made sure of that. It all happened. What was done was done. I suppose. The more he explained, the more clarity he offered, the less concrete it seemed.

To experience what didn't happen is to become acquainted with a shard of probable history. Something we don't know we're neglecting and try very hard not to remember. It didn't happen therefore it's wise and true. It didn't happen therefore it stands before us, existing. If we imagined it, it happened before or will happen later. Anything imagined is possible because that's how it could be, seen with the right evidence. Anything imagined is definite if an expert thought so or if a recorded narrative claimed. Every sick, horrific thought you committed exists out there. In fact every fear, however irrational or unlikely, has played out somewhere, somehow, because it was imagined. I know this because my daddy told me so. My father inspired a number of my most striking prospective memories.

Daddy, if I cut your throat, what would pour forth?

"When your mother cut my throat, it was creamy pearls and teeth. She strung a necklace from them. She said it was the first nice thing she ever got from me. I reminded her that I had nothing nice to offer, but that one time she seemed genuinely appreciative," my father said with a partial smile that wasn't entirely unnerving, but certainly wasn't what one would call warm, "I'm curious what your slice will bring forth. Have you ever considered it?"

I'm nothing like my mother.

"Of course you aren't. Except that you bear a striking resemblance, and your voice is very similar and of course your penchant for thump and terror."

Said the bomb maker.

"Touché! But why not Bomb Father? Haven't I earned it? I believe I have and now my work is finished. I'm tired, my sun is setting and I have no son to murder and replace me. It's all so utterly disappointing."

I will kill you, Father.

"I know you will, my love, but it's just not the legacy I envisioned. My name can't carry through a daughter. Even if she did keep it, her children would get another man's. Not that you ever bothered to gift me any grandchildren. You've shown a striking lack of ambition. But I think it's adorable that you're going to make the effort. Maybe you could write a poem about me and my philanthropy? You could submit it to one of those *Best Of* anthologies. That could be something you could do."

I couldn't even force a smile. He must have noticed my disappointment, the hurt I could no longer mask. He seemed proud of that. Some might see irony in his philanthropy. All I saw were worms moving on to a new carcass.

"There, there, darling, show Daddy what you learned over the decades. Show Daddy the ways a woman can make her name in this man's world. Prove me wrong. Prove to me that you could sustain and build on my legacy better than any man could dream. Wouldn't it be valuable to your sense of worth for me to acknowledge that I underestimated you all these years?" His snorts and sarcasm thick with truth, "Time is running out for you to be appreciated. Perhaps your problem is that you were never cut out for womanhood? Perhaps you'd be more successful in drag? Have you considered what your drag name might be? 'Daddy's Little Bombmaker'?"

Here Father was creating his own historical record. His name meant nothing to me, so little in fact, I don't remember it. I didn't remember it then. To me he was just "Daddy." But no one will record that, so that's not part of this memory.

But take it from me, his name, like his acknowledgement, was worthless. Less than worthless. Yet this worthlessness was my measurement for everything.

It would also be unlikely for it to be discovered that this murder was a KIND murder. I believed that as the daughter of a bomb maker, enduring his philanthropy, I earned a blank slate and the opportunity to create my own system of measurement. I was never going to get that as long as he kept adding onto his legacy. His legacy cursed my inheritance.

Disgusting fucking bombs!

"Hey now, those bombs put food on our table and paid for your college," he said pushing the plate with the pill towards me.

Then I understood what he was explaining in his insidious, manipulative fashion. This was the pill to make it all go away and start over. This was the bomb to end bombs. Even if he wouldn't admit it.

Boomba.

In one hand I held the pill. In the other a jagged blade, with an exquisite pearl handle.

I swallowed it. The pill to kill. A pill that was a bomb that triggered the slice. I had no intention of continuing my father's philanthropy. I just didn't want to be her and he linked me to her, another curse I needed to blank.

There will be no pearl necklace for me, my foul, beloved patriarch.

Did I hesitate? Not for a moment. Was I frightened? No, but I should have been. Slicing my father's throat brought forth a menagerie of creatures tearing through his Adam's apple, many I couldn't identify. So many, I lost count. They kept coming through the neck smoke, humanoids and animals and blobs and worms, some much too large to fit through the slice in his neck, but somehow they came through. A ferret riding on an elk with multiple stab wounds. A blue dog barking "white cat." A dying fox gasping "Oh my Pompeii." A lanky reaper-type. A cow wearing zebra print. A lizard in leopard. Another lizard wearing a feather boa. A monkey selling laundry soap. A graffiti-covered snail. My mother, neglecting to acknowledge my presence, in every size and shape and color imaginable. A trick-or-treating goat. A parrot with a vendetta. A dodo in a top hat. A deflated whale trying to breathe. Donkey driving a speedboat like an assbeast. Fairies dressed as Furries. Furries masquerading as authorities. Wraiths in Garanimals. A brown fish choking on a silver cigar. A five foot penis accompanied by his charmed rape riddles. Pasta Primavera served with a hangnail. A crying raccoon cradling a limp snakeskin. An animal control van with the driver hanging out the window screaming, "I'm going to get you, my feral, and your little bird too."

Then out came the clowns, clowns in business attire, clowns pushing baby carriages, clowns before chalkboards, pregnant clowns, clowns with bayonets, clowns in scrubs, clowns in beakers, crammed clowns riding on top of a tiny alligator, clowns with their attorneys, clowns with tinsel and worms blowing out their asses.

There were sounds, many loud and few soft, all excruciating in pitch, some hurt my teeth and then there were sensations, pulsations, shivers, chills and sweats. For a second I felt like I grew a massive erection, but that quickly passed. I lost my sense of place and time and the loss kept coming, wrapped in a big fat flatworm.

It felt rejuvenating to be without loss until I began to think about what I was losing out on by not having it.

Unsigned Note from Yonder

On the tinseled turds of elks
a thumping arrived
without a name.
This tragic parasite
writhing
for a breath or
admonishment.
What's in its
stomach
is a liar.
What's in its
mouth
can be persuaded.

Symposium on 21st Century Culture

MODERATOR: For our next example we consider the remains of a man, roughly 70 years of age at his death. His death was the result of a very deep laceration across his throat with a knife. After the cut was made, the knife remained stuck, possibly intentionally abandoned, in his throat. Genetic testing shows that the murderer was the man's own biological daughter (approximately 37-42 years old). A number of interesting questions arise. The most obvious, why did she slit her father's throat? Was she prosecuted in the court of law at the time? Was it a murderous rage? Was it in self-defense? Was it a ritual sacrifice? Did she hesitate? How did she feel afterwards? Why did she leave the knife in his neck? Why were no tears found on the knife? Did she not love her father?

ARCHAEOLOGIST: The knife remained in his throat because she was too weak to pull it out. 21st century women lost their upper-body strength after pole dancing went out of fashion and evolved into what can be best described as fat-bottomed Tyrannosaurs. The cut was symbolic of her no longer relying on her father for support. When a father's purpose ends, it was common practice for his children to end his life. She did not cry because it was not a sad event, but a coming of age ritual. She simply carried on the tradition of the time. No doubt a proud moment for the father to see his adult daughter finally reach independence. At her advanced age, he likely waited a long time for this moment to finally happen.

HISTORIAN: The knife was purposely left in his throat because that was the way of the religious sect called Freud that identified themselves with phalluses. This act was an intentional violation of all the words to ever originate from his larynx. It is likely that this murder stemmed from a lover's quarrel since father/daughter sexual relations were common and acceptable at the time in this sect. She didn't cry because she had already cried earlier when she first learned of his betrayal. These incestuous relationships were always based on a betrayal, first the mother, then the daughter, then the next daughter or the son, if there ever was one which there probably wasn't judging by the father being such a tremendous failure. I propose that the knife was a symbol of the father's penis usurped by his daughter. She penetrated him with his own power because her envy made her powerless to do otherwise.

SCUBA DIVER: There is little evidence of consensual father/daughter sexual relationships during the 21st century, even in the Freudian cults which were mostly composed of people who just liked to sit around and talk about such things. What was rampant was molestation and abuse. We can't say for sure whether this was a case of molestation or some other long-term fatherly abuse. My best guess leads me to suggest a revenge murder, also common and promoted within the Bronson and Borden cults. She didn't cry because she'd been submerged in the idea since birth. She did not hesitate because she'd been trained to hold her breath. Inspired by the feminist poetry of her time, she decided that her life's purpose was to learn how to breathe differently, anonymously. She couldn't be anonymous carrying around her father's knife in her pocket. When she finished cutting his throat, putting an end, once and for all, to his laborious breaths, all what was left for her to do was to cut all ties to him.

ARCHIVIST: There are no records of a biological daughter therefore she didn't exist and therefore could not have killed her father. We believe the man, who certainly was no father, slit his own throat. Probably because he failed to produce an heir for his sterile legacy. He ended it because he was already finished. No park bench named for him. Another forgotten slab for the heap.

Recovered Memory

When we entered the party the butler handed us each a twinkling carrot, the custom before an excavation, the symbol of enticement. Enticement was necessary because these excavations always began in the same dank childhood basement hoarded with bric-a-brac indicating you were a catalyst for violence, that you caused harm and brought violence and death for your own petty benefit. It went back, it went deep, dark and full of spiders, spinning and waiting to snare you. A fertile thing going thump in your gut. Selfdom as a roulette wheel. Selfdom like a hula hoop. Clay. A new dance craze twirling you around until you're paralyzed by the stains that reflect you from all angles.

"Stay out of the basement, creatures tend to clash when they reconstruct and oh gosh, the smell, you don't want a whiff of that smell. You'll carry that stench with you for the rest of your time, and afterward you'll forget it," said the grayish party guest who did his best to impress me with his disappearing orb trick.

"Try the attic, it's slower-going, sleepier, dryer and there's a lot more room to spread out, bring up what you like, convert it into something that reaches a legitimate keepsake status. That way it'll retain its value and you can pass it on without fear of mold. It's a consumer's market out there and consumers don't want mold in anything, growing, tainting the biological structure."

Something About Birds

There is always, always, a dead bird at the bottom of every woman.

Lily told me as much after I threw up and held the small, brown creature in my palms. The final thing to emerge after I sliced his throat and swallowed the pill. Seconds after I swallowed, I realized I didn't really want this gift and knew I should have stopped while ahead. There was nothing forcing me to swallow the pill. No one around. My father dead. Why didn't I just walk away from his corpse and menagerie? What a dreadful gift and what a curse to desire it, if only for a moment. I changed my mind and didn't want to inherit any of this. What I really wanted was to be left alone, in peace. And understood. And accepted. Being loved as is would have been a big plus. But I tricked myself thinking I could get what I desired from an exploding pill passed down from my father.

Why didn't I just walk away and start fresh on my own?

Because I was a dingbat and it was too late. Everything set itself in motion. First I coughed up pieces of the wine glass I used to wash down the pill. Rather frightening, considering I didn' intend to consume the glass or remember it, but I got through it and soon felt a mistaken relief thinking that would be it. Until up came the old equipment I cleaned out of my basement earlier that month. How did these outdated routers and peripherals get inside me, cords and all? I didn't remember eating them either, but somehow these broken machines wedged in real deep, followed by partially digested food, maybe cat food considering that it looked like something I cleaned off the floor countless times before. Fast-acting, sinking mountains of cat barf. At that point I got so used to choking up the cat-like vomit it became almost normal and comforting.

Until it was followed by the bird.

Look what the cat dragged into me. Was this supposed to be my soul? A bird flies, did that make it spirit? Masculine or feminine? My animal urge? Was this what I had in myself? Was this what I had to work with? Was it really dead? If so, for how long? Was it alive before the pill bomb? Could I miss what I didn't know and never met? Should I be faulted for my ignorance? Mocked? Pitied? Naturalized? Appropriated? Accepted?

The dead bird as new terrain with no map or guidebook.

In hindsight, I should have realized that swallowing the pill would open me up and unearth all sorts of terrible things. My father warned it wouldn't be nice.

And Lily? All this time I thought she spoke in metaphor.

Or rather, I hoped.

"There is always, always, a dead bird at the bottom of every woman."

Except for me, not now, at least. I coughed up my dead bird and yes, I was shocked to see it, shocked it was there, even though there is one at the bottom of every woman and I was a woman.

Did I not know? Did I forget? Did I ever know? Now that I knew, could I pretend I didn't? Could I continue living without a dead bird at my bottom? I missed what I hadn't known I possessed and this pill wouldn't let me forget, just as it insisted I swallow it. Fate in pill form and powerless against it. I roofied myself. This pill insisted I do something about this dead bird. I must not have paid attention because I immediately forgot what I was supposed to do with it. Maybe get another dead bird? Or give birth to the dead bird? Would that bring it back? Or was I supposed to find a new living bird? Was I supposed to bury the bird in a pet cemetery haunted by forgotten spirits who were not yet at rest? Completely confusing, yet I just knew I needed to take this dead bird somewhere and do something with it.

This pill didn't just bomb my insides, it made demands, set a new will into motion, set off firecrackers in small animals' asses. This wild vicious bomb and its new internal order. Shit was mixed up, churning, and I felt frothy.

And vulnerable.

I feared this bomb-dictated excavation. No doubt the deeper I got, the worse it would be. The men would grope me. The women would stand by their groping men, call me weird for crying and deny record of their many hands pawing, probing my parts, sacred, vile and leaking. Men punishing first, then questioning, ladies punishing next, snickering like dragons and holding a parade of sneers and relics in my dishonor

Then those fuckers would all tweet and retweet and favorite and fuck them, I wasn't going near them.

Um would go in my place, I thought. These circumstances were precisely why I married. When there's a varmit giving birth in the chimney, I would turn to Um's varmit-midwife expertise to light a fire and smoke that life right out. Why shouldn't he venture into this Bombyonder for me? His stomach could hold so much more than mine, he wouldn't even notice one small, feathered corpse. He could travel to birth the bird corpse without a squawk, without a peep, without a vagina. So tall and muscled, it would have been so easy for him. His long, hairy legs would carry him in half the time. No one would grope a giant, no one would stand by and call him weird or accuse him of frothing lies, flinging shingles. Giants in respect to Titans in respect to *it's what's for dinner come on in and have a seat.* Then the ladies would lavish him with food and their bodily gifts, support and help him murder an old hag for her magical bird, an old hag they once lunched with until she started to fade.

The world works as the world works. Nothing we can do about that.

His quest would be the hero's on behalf of a distant princess stuck in a tower, or a shower, or most likely this princess will be stuck in bed with the flu because like I said, there was a lot of froth spewing forth. Something certainly wasn't right inside me.

While my prince, fixed my fallout, this distant princess stuck in her bed, would surf to somewhere splendid to update her belly cage. I'd start on Etsy in safety, working on my tasks in private, spinning poems into gold, counting poems into gold, shitting gold and calling it "my glad little calling" to spread on my daily bread, amen.

I knew what side my bread was golden-shat on.

When Um returned with my new bird, I'd be ready. I'd say, *Thank you my manly bird catcher. Present my new bird to receive your reward, my hand in what could only be a higher plane of marriage. I've been home, waiting, nesting for this very moment.*

Happily ever after he would take out the garbage and recyclables piling in the kitchen, remove the dead mouse from the trap and open that stubborn jar of spaghetti sauce.

Everything would return to right.

Go for me. Find me a bird. I begged Um, *I would be in your debt. I would make it worth your while. When you return I won't even ask what you did with all those lavishing ladies' body parts you'll certainly be offered. I won't judge. I won't nag. Just please go and do this for me.*

I wailed and trailed Um around our home, chugged and chooed like a cheerleader circling a majorette closing for a bloodsported inning. How could he say no to my simple, humble needs? Did I not go to his tribe's homes, celebrate their holidays, eat their ham-filled foods? Did I not bite my tongue when he mocked my father? Did I not plug my ears when he snickered at my mother? When he belittled all things bombish and lady-ish, did I not let it all drizzle down my back like foamish ostrich shit without even a twitch? Didn't I?

I most certainly did.

Um disagreed. Denied me in every way imaginable, he denied every request. He wanted nothing of my dead bird, wouldn't even hear of it. He said it wasn't for him to do, but for me.

He said he was tired of being my go-to manbitch.

If you don't do this for me, we're kaput. Wiped out. Your refusal irretrievably wrecks our marriage. I will rain tears of napalm and you will never fuck again. That I will guarantee.

I think I meant it too.

"To love, honor and destroy is your tribe's way, not mine." he said, asking for it, he of birdlessness. He who accepted every taunt and quest but mine.

Please, I'll be raped in twenty rooms, on slabs, on altars, on futons and daybeds, by old men and goblins and football teams and mascots, by strangers and familiars, photographed and ridiculed by harpies and matrons, they'll photoshop me pore by pore and those images will spread until the end of the universe. How could you let that happen to your own wife?

That may have been an exaggeration. For all I knew it could have been far fewer rooms. It could all happen in one big cavern. I'd never been to a bombsite or below, but I knew what I could imagine and what I could imagine was rather gruesome. Better for a man to go for me. I could imagine a much safer experience for Um than I could ever imagine for myself. The only reasonable way, I was sure. Um just needed to reflect on my request again, or so I thought. I really thought he'd come around. Um never denied me before.

What was to be was that I found a gun in the basement and shot Um twice in the chest full of what I never imagined, but someone else must have imagined because it was there before me, Um with a chest shot full of metal or lead or whatever it was that I blasted into him. It's not like I ever looked inside the loaded gun. It's not like I understood the inner mechanics. All I need to know in this world was pull the trigger and BOOMBA.

He fell down quite dead, without a single doubt, from the cold bullets from my burning palm. I checked for his pulse. Performed mouth-to-mouth. No use. I was of no use to Um, the slab of once-my-husband. Nothing left to do but call the police and claim that I thought he was a burglar disguised as my husband.

Being a professor's daughter meant I would be treated as reliable. I could be convincing as a dingbat. All I needed was a little time to practice my shakes and tears in front of a mirror.

So I was surprised when Um resurrected behind my reflection and positively shocked when he apologized, acknowledged my fears, feelings and broken expectations.

"You must have felt very frightened and alone. You must have felt disappointed and betrayed."

Oh man, did I ever!

I still do feel frightened and alone, disappointed and betrayed, but I appreciate your acknowledging it.

Where was my husband, the one I just murdered? I never imagined such a transformation, or perhaps I did once in the guise of a fantasy. Death changed him into a gorgeous, sensitive creature straight from an unapologetic chick flick. Was this a comparable result to a kind bomb? Had I my father's fingers, his touch with his kindness? I never wanted Um more than I did right at that moment as I experienced an unanticipated marital nostalgia.

You are now so much better than the man I always loved. Such a spectacular improvement. All I had to do was shoot you. I do believe death transformed you into my soul mate. Let's start over again and spend the rest of our lives together. We'll go to Bombyonder together. It'll be like a second honeymoon. It'll be romantic.

"Yes, transformation tends to follow death. Now that I don't exist, I qualify to be your soul mate. I am so very sorry for making you shoot me. We both were trying to be right. I was trying to get you to do something for yourself and you were trying to get me to do the task you accepted for yourself but were trying to worm out. Now I know I was doing it wrong. But sadly, my delicate nest, this is to truly be our end just the same," he said as he stroked my hair as he never stroked before.

Sadly, Um was right. Soul mate or not, whether he fit the qualifications or not, there is no future with a corpse.

Yes, I'm afraid that this is our end. If we tried to stay together you would find another way to make me shoot you. It's inevitable. As long as you exist trying to make me take this responsibility I reject, I will keep killing you. Forgive me, I took a pill that was a bomb that weaponized me. I'm afraid I will kill at a blink—out of a necessary mercy. You are right, it is the way of my tribe.

"Of course. You can't stop your killing. Every speck of you is consumed by a murderous rage. Killing always prevails and your tribe is the tribe that prevails, your cold, colonizing tufts of paste go back to the beginning of the written word, maybe even cave paintings. Softly, hardly, in the end it's all killing for the glory of yourselves. Nothing you can do but build history on our backs, take it upon yourselves to bestow significance and select what is to be a souvenir. Don't weep for me, my shriveled dodo. Never give me another thought. The gods created me for the specific purpose of being the means to your end. Go out, jump in a swamp and don't stop sinking until you reach your bottom, my sad, catastrophic wife."

Um left, murdered and shiftless, without taking my death bird to birth, without so much as a farewell kiss. When he said this was our end, I believed he really meant it and resented him for it. Dead for such a short time and already so dreadfully annoying with his victim mentality.

I was glad he was gone. Even though his body remained, saddling me with more weight.

And I, bombed and endowed, stared at the feathered corpse resting in my freshly murdering palm. Not knowing where to go next.

What was I to do? What could I do?

Nothing. I refused. I didn't move. I would not go anywhere. I would not. I did not.

I didn't have to.

The bombsite consumed me.

First Induced Memory

When we slowmo-drifted to the silent casino to spend our hard earned ghoulishness, our boat needed something specific to cut through the ice created from the methodic chomping of alligators.

We possessed so few specifics with our pockets full of pearls and teeth. Weren't there any schematics or blueprints or subterranean planners?

We needed coins and slips and we needed help drawing a blank and we needed to do it here before here was printed and sold to scuba divers and archivists.

Slots were hard on a body, on a door, on the ear, on a belief system. All the empty slots ironically filled with junk, winning and losing it all with each pull.

A silent casino was not a good place for sleeping or rowing, so quiet all you could do was think about the teeth cutting through your ass.

What to avoid: sharp edges, a full drawer of records, masked pageant preparations, whales, thumping funnels spewing bloodworms.

What needed to be done needed to be done and this now would be a time for a renovation, reboot, an inspirational quote, pee break, an appointment lending attention to that still needing attention.

The things we lost: a feather, an orb, parrot, cat, donkey, status, privacy, Heath Ledger, our lice.

Reflection brought the freeze, I looked and it all stopped, I counted, I wept, I preserved, I slept.

I woke practically a reptile.

Court Transcript

SUPERIOR COURT OF BOMBYONDER
CASE: Bombyonder vs. (fill in blank)
DATE: (fill in blank)

    THE COURT: Please begin with opening arguments.
    PROSECUTION: Ladies and Gentleman of the Jury, I want to talk to you like human beings because the characters involved here are honest-to-goodness people, albeit some are dead honest-to-goodness people. The case before you is about humanity. Who has ownership of it? Does the defendant have any? Can someone so utterly unlikable be worthy of it?
    Carl Jung once asked, "Do women have souls?"
    The internet avatar by the name of "Macaroni" claims in the comment field, "Women are the stupid men who were born without penises." He has a point, does he not? Few women are born with penises, true? And if women were so smart, wouldn't they have more impressive legacies? The avatar "Bologna" furthers this assertion by adding, "Not only do women not have souls, they will suck the very soul out of any man who gives them a chance!" Suck indeed.

What else has the defendant sucked at?

This brings up the next point. Can the defendant ever be likable? Can we scrounge any empathy for this murderer of men? This eater of legacies? This disrespecter of tradition and order?

We have before us a defendant, a spiteful woman without a penis of her own, who when given the chance to steal the souls of two men, her own husband and father, she took it. Without hesitation. The fact that we're here today stands to reason that she is a chance taker. Where are their souls? What has been done with them?

You'll have to ask the defendant.

It is my belief that if given additional opportunity, she will take a great deal more solely for the benefit of her own soulless self. Ladies of the Jury, perhaps you feel safe or unmoved because the defendant's history up to this point only includes the murders of men. Perhaps you can identify with aspects of the defendant? Perhaps your father neglected and dismissed you? Perhaps you've had a less than stellar boyfriend or a husband who passed gas in his sleep? Perhaps you can make some sort of depraved sense of her reasoning? To that I say, don't be such ridiculous ninnies. She doesn't like you either and when she's finished working through your men, she'll come for you. And when that happens, there will be no big, strong men left to protect and stand up for your honor or your lives. You will be alone and likely old and unattractive, probably in the midst of your "change" as you are left on your lonesome.

Remember that, ladies. A misanthrope hates all humankind and whether you realize it or not, humankind includes you too.

Aftermath: The Reluctant and Homicidal Heroine Seeks What She Does Not Want

First I noticed one of her arms was missing, as my grandmother pushed me in a wheelbarrel to the mouth of Bombyonder. That was too bad, if I remembered correctly, that was her good arm that got blasted away. Still, my grandmother wasn't one to complain and silently managed, one-armed, to push me to a sunken crater, littered with shards of hard candy, cracked grandfather clocks, iPods, curlers, magazines, faded hats, scarves, awkward purses and other in-demand accessories. Bombyonder looked like a bomb leveled an entire world created as a backdrop for a far-off science fiction novel that took place in an outlet mall. When the wind blew from the north it smelled like a barnyard crossed with a zoo on a sultry noon day. From the west, the breeze smelled distinctly like a urinal mint that took on more urine than it could manage. This place felt like a trendy Soho-style loft converted from an abandoned funeral parlor.

From her tattered apron my grandmother pulled out two items: a crystal orb with the word "smart" etched onto it and a pencil with the message: "A is for Ass".

I don't know why she bothered passing on this brittle legacy. Surely her death a decade ago would have been sufficient excuse to sit out this blitzkrieg. Tribal loyalty perhaps. Maybe boredom. Perhaps this was an unexpected opportunity for her to right a legacy long ignored. Or perhaps this was her investment in future tribal output. To live on in the DNA of descendants. Everybody wants to cement their position in the rubble, even if it's just a name on a cracked, shared tombstone.

Everybody but me.

I couldn't think on it much longer. Stressed about participating in this dig and reconstruction, too stressed to consider motivations, too stressed to remember if she was my paternal or maternal grandmother. Was she the one who insisted I memorize prayers for the dinner table or the one who insisted that one could never be too rich or too thin? My family tree was a series of vines entangled over a long-abandoned church. A tree I wished would burn down, but lately I suspected it was eternal and damned.

My suspicions prompted more questions. Did my grandmother expect a postcard written of memories to come? A well-thought and handwritten thank you? Was I to name my next bird after her so she could live on in something? Was I expected to memorialize this moment with a photograph or tweet? Did she just load me down with her own psychic crap to make herself lighter? What are the ethics of forgetting one's ancestors? Was it my debt to take out her garbage? Was that my inheritance? I trusted no one's motivation, especially not the motivations little old ladies related to me. We weren't derived from a nurturing stock.

Thank you for the unwanted gifts. I will cherish them like a Sunday afternoon watching broadcast channels on your black and white TV.

She nodded her head, but didn't speak or even smile, not even a little.

Because she didn't have her lower jaw. That's why she didn't tell me to start praying or suggest I make a few more trips to the salad bar. That's why my barrel ride was so blissfully silent. I probably should have noticed earlier but was distracted with my bird corpse and urge to obliterate anything that got too close. Or tried to run. Or smirked.

What people don't realize is that the mouth of Bombyonder looks like a ferry of staircase mazes built of traveling trunks that a long-dead god crapped out. There was no semblance of intelligent design. The ferry never seemed to leave the dock. For all I knew it wasn't even a boat. It could have been a mausoleum. It smelled like a mausoleum: marbled, putrified meat mingling with Chanel No. 5.

I boarded the ferry without argument because it was preferable to spending more of the afternoon staring at my silent, decaying, blasted grandmother. I boarded with my gifted baggage, sat at a table on the deck for a good long time, weighed down by maternal kitsch. I ordered a really large glass of water:

Big honking-ass glass of water, on the double!

The waiter replied, "Who you calling a honky, honky?" and mocked my request by giving me a glass filled an inch high.

I berated the waiter, then berated my water and then drank my inch of water. I tipped poorly. I paced the ferry, looked over the rail, out into the horizon, spat on a slutty-looking mermaid who looked a lot like some ho I used to know, visited the gift shop, not buying any of the Gibsonian riddles:

"What do women REALLY want?"

It wasn't kindness, that was for sure. My father possessed and distributed all the kindness and certainly was no lady magnet.

Back-biting ogress magnet, maybe.

THIS WOMAN WANTS TO BE LEFT ALONE.

THIS WOMAN WANTS TO BE AN ORPHAN TO ANCESTRY.

THIS WOMAN DOESN'T WANT TO BE BOTHERED WITH THE BOMBYONDER.

I sulked, squinted and finally relented to go-time. I ascended the spiral staircase imitating the boat center to take me somewhere almost, but never quite, long lost to myself.

On the top step sat a little girl creature with a blue face. She looked liked a parrot with the face of a cat. A squawking mini-feminine, adorable in a her human aspects, disconcerting from afar. She conjured a type of trepidation that slowly evolved into a serene familiarity. She stood two steps up from me and touched my face. Surprisingly, I didn't flinch or scream. Usually I'm bothered when people go near my face. Maybe it was OK because she was more like a parrot-cat than a human being.

To my relief, I felt no urge to murder her. Just a pleasant tingling and a low, peaceful buzz.

My breathing slowed, my grip on the dead-vomit bird loosened. This must be what it felt like to be relaxed. But I prepared for something else. This parrot-girl looked sweet, but I didn't trust her. She had to be more than she seemed. I liked the idea of her but didn't feel the emotional investment to try to understand her feelings and concerns. Just by looking at her I could tell that she was teeming with needs and emotions. I guess you could say that I was content to make her acquaintance but didn't much care to get to know her.

She gestured for me to go down the stairs then pointed at a mural of leopards, lizards and wolves as if that was a sign instructing me what to do.

Leopards and lizards and wolves, oh my!

Yeah, I mocked her. It was a long time since I chuckled and guffawed, seemed like a waste to pass up this opportunity to laugh at a ridiculous blue creature. Then it occurred to me that perhaps this blue girl could be of some help placing my dead bird and retrieving a suitable replacement. While she didn't say, she seemed to want to help. Or at least that's how I interpreted the situation through her appearance and action. So being both smart and an ass, I scooped the blue girl up in my arms and told her she was coming with me. Everyone knew the little Bombyonder orphans were the best guides of all, especially the girls with their nimble creature minds. My father's menagerie told me that much.

A few steps down the blue girl pointed to the railing, motioned that I was on the wrong side of it. I tried to straddle the railing and switch sides. My footing unsteady, the stairs rickety, not helped by the animal menagerie stampede below. THUMPING PSYCHIC MENAGIER. I couldn't keep my grip but this wasn't a problem for long because soon a huge wave knocked me completely off the staircase. In my gasping and flailing, the blue girl slipped from my grasp.

I panicked, did I already lose my guide? My mini-doula? My fast track to ending this descent? Why did I always mock the help?

I gulped water, calling for her to return. Couldn't see anything through the mist. Couldn't hear anything over the churning of my stomach. Thought for sure I would die before recovering anything more than this lacking and I certainly would have, if it were not for a hand from below pulling me down deeper.

On the other side of the water, the hand belonged to a woman in heels and high hair, broad shoulder pads. A smaller version of myself trying to seem big, it seemed. Also I seemed to be in the lobby of a lovely upscale hotel. Recovery from an almost drowning was a lovely upscale hotel with many portraits of less-than-attractive individuals hanging on the walls with inspirational messages like "Hang in There, Ho!" and "You Can Do It, Necrophiliac!" and "A Leper is a Launderer of Lies."

Everyone had potential here, it seemed, and for the first time I was feeling a bit hopeful. Honestly, all I knew of non-existent memories was what I read in magazines and heard from my father. For there was never a myth or historical text without his editorial hand. Are his hands on the designs of this lobby? Did my father still possess hands? Or did the pill bomb blow them off like Grandma's arm and jaw? Could I be so fortunate?

I could live here forever!

I really believed I could live in this clean, non-judgmental place. I could learn to forgive all sorts of things in a place like this, or at least stop thinking of them. Maybe I could even learn to like people, appreciate their humanity. For the first time in a while I didn't feel like killing anyone.

Not even smothering someone with a pillow while she snored.

Here must be where memories are collected and safely filed away to be later put on display. Like a museum.

"No this isn't and no you can't stay here much longer. There's a limit and you've almost reached it," my 2/3 version replied. "Where is your home? Do you remember a basement? Did you see the drawers? Did you open any of them? Do you know what's inside?"

I told her about my house, the basement where I shot Um, my father and his bombs. I left out the part about slitting his throat because while this place might seem non-judgmental, you never really know. Nothing is what it seems. I asked if she saw a blue-faced girl. I didn't mention a mother. I explained how these days I was more interested in attics. As I spoke it felt like my stomach was expanding with gas. Like it could blow at any time.

    She shook her head. That wasn't what she was asking, but I didn't have an answer because I didn't really understand the question. "Where is my home?" is like asking "Who am I?" or "Why am I here?" Or "What is my purpose?" There aren't really truths to those questions, just perceptions passed on as legacies. If you go back far enough, you'll discover every indigenous group descended from immigrants. As it turns out, we didn't come from anywhere. There is no universal agreement on pretty much anything, I was sure. Only a universal sense of burden. I have a tribe. When it was about Father, it was about Father. When it was about Mother, it was about Mother. When it was about me, it wasn't. It was about how I fucked everything up for everyone else. My home wasn't about me either. It's where I was placed, by others, for their own reasons.

    "You are in luck because you reached Bombyonder and can start over from a new beginning."

    Smaller Me took me to my room draped in faded denim. In what year did people wear this denim and what would it mean to try it on now? Would the seams hold? Now I had choices, I could use the denim as my garment to inhabit, to protect and serve. Or I could use the denim as my papyrus, stretch it out as a canvas to be the foundation on which to record and build. Or I could bedazzle and cut the denim into strips then hot glue them onto the frame of the mirror before me. I could hot glue denim strips on everything and open an upscale resale shop. I could start by hot gluing something over the original message of the pencil given to me by my grandmother. I could make it something completely different.

    A is for APHRODISIAC.

    A is for APOCALYPSE.

    A is for ACTUALLY NOT GONNA HAPPEN.

    I could make it like that pencil never existed. I could make it a back scratcher or shoe horn. Does anyone really know much about the foundation on which they stand? Is it even necessary?

    I was thinking not so much.

    I could cover Um's corpse in denim. I could decoupage and superimpose an entirely new lover overtop his failures. One of my own image, the image I create for him. A handsome, feminist bad boy who brooded deep thoughts and ambition.

    A is for ADONIS.

    A is for ABOMINATION.

    A is for ADAM'S APPLE.

    A is for ALAS.

Unrecovered Memories

I can't remember the end of a single summer or the first school bell of the year, the beginnings, the ends, vanished, leaving only the smudged assignments, uncompleted.

I can't remember which events happened before, after or during the bombing.

I can't remember reaching a single foreign land, yet I have shoeboxes full of pictures and travel logs.

I can't remember when brown didn't taste like red.

I can't remember the place where I used to throw up, but the piles and mountains of vomit surround me, blocking my view.

I can't remember a simple ending of a past war—have any ever successfully ended?

I can't remember what it was like caring for a single him or what it was like being cared for by a single her.

I can't remember my love, but I remember sitting under the weeping willow waiting for it to return.

I can't remember not being a dingbat.

I can't remember erasing my face or if it was just a typo erasing my fate instead.

I can't remember if the Artist Formerly Known as Prince ever really existed or if I simply desired him to exist.

I can't remember giving the porter my shoes or where I asked him to stick them.

Recovered Memory

We inherited a lake with a house complete with a breeze and a frozen compartment filled with wealth and games. What to keep, what to carry in our hearts and what to carry in our guts. What to give away. What to sell and what to let sink. What to expect. What to do with such things. I inherited photographs that I kept out of respect for something I had no respect for and would never display.

Unframed, the lake was an enormous glacier melting. Framed, the lake was a swamp.

There's a basic formula you need to know when going into a swamp, otherwise it's something unexpected. Otherwise it's too depressing upon recovering the bloated deliveries floating on the surface. Otherwise there would be handling and bobbing and gulping. Otherwise you'd have to look and once you saw, you remembered what was dumped there to be forgotten.

Otherwise you'd have to acknowledge it all and after you acknowledged, you'd be expected to learn something from it, avoid repeating.

I couldn't recall the basic formula but I remembered there was life to be found in a swamp.

Murky.
Fetid.
Bloated life.

Introduction to Terror

Presented with the reflection of my labors, I gazed at my miscreation. This was not Um and certainly not my father.

Who was he?

Three generations of stud wrapped in one ball of flesh coated with the finest vintage denim. The source of all the world's hot glue, dribbling, his lamblike testicles sautéed in butter and chives nestled over a bed of lettuce. A succulent slab with a long history of mnemonic cannibalism. A primitive metrosexual in search of explosives and I came from a long line of fuses.

Oh, he was my equal all right.

Without hesitation I rested in his hairy embrace and quickly sunk into the groping. Love at last sight.

Here you are, all mine. I am your creator. You came from my pencil and denim, spun around a future passed away, in a hail of bullets, now studded and bedazzled. You shall inherit Bombyonder. All these shards and rubble are yours to use to build a new way with me.

I took my role as creator very seriously.

The only way to describe him would be terrifyingly handsome. Another way might be charming as a butcher block.

When you want to run away and fuck at the same time, when you first meet your creation, you know there's something behind the persona, the meat and flesh, past the tonsils, down the throat, swimming in the future regurgitation. There's something more, but you don't connect the dots. You don't think too deeply because only you realize there's no turning back from such knowledge that you can neither turn back or completely bury.

Or at least, I couldn't turn back once I gazed upon his seductive, grim form.

He's breathing.

You enjoy the brutality of all the senses.

As you should.

I understand, I enjoyed it all at first too.

Vomit it up all you can, but that awful something is already absorbed, already part of the body, the landscape, the equation. It's science, it's art, it's the math you never attempted to learn but somehow you absorbed the concept and thank God you did otherwise you wouldn't be able to breathe down here because this guy is burning up all the air.

We invented forgetting millions ago because we thought it was possible, more attainable than flying, turning invisible or forgiving the ones who wronged us. At least we didn't go so far as to pretend we could heal. At least we should be credited with that.

Forgetting was not disappearing, it was burial and after enough time passed what was buried began to chemically break down, parts disintegrated, what was buried changed, sometimes melding with its surroundings, sometimes poisoning. Sometimes something new would sprout from it and that could very well be anything but it was always unexpected. The more we buried, the more our forgetting accumulated, the deeper it went, millions of years deep, perhaps more, we don't know how many layers it goes. If we did, we forgot. What we know now is that no matter how decayed, there are always remnants and the remnants are never just remnants—they're the Styrofoam of the soul.

But we don't recall it as Styrofoam. We're nostalgic. We name it Bakelite while associating it with the aroma of blackberry muffins cooling in the shadows of a waning moon. This all consuming, limitless landfill is the hole in our bellies. We try to reconnect and remember when we were children brutalized by other children who were being brutalized by the same adults who were brutalizing us. Simpler times when all you needed to know was that you were at the mercy of the worthy's whims. We yearn to recreate our horrors into tchotchkes and hey everyone, get your free swag.

No honor in nostalgia.

No, there's honor codes, pledges, honor and duty, honor rolls, societies, honor among thieves, honor killings.

Honor thy mother and father. Stay in school. Stay nostalgic.

When I saw my creation the first thing he reminded me was that the blood on my hands never washed because my hands are full of blood. I built with blood and destroyed with blood. It started, it ended, and all throughout, always blood. What other way was there?

Who did he look like most?

Well, he would have had his father's eyes, if he had a father.

He had my father's eyes?

I think not.

Were his eyes like mine?

Well, it's tough to say, annihilation ran on both sides of my family.

My parents had very promising futures, much like how their parents had promising futures. So many promises at their fingertips. How else to survive if not to accept the role of apologist and continue the tradition? There is no way to survive otherwise. I forget that I forgot. I preferred to forget my corrupted incubuses.

Um's corpse as my mother's patchwork quilt.

No, pig in a denim-studded blanket.

I am the creator. For the first time I can design my destiny.

That's what I told myself.

There is No Plan or Sense

All this nostalgic creation lead me to speculate on retrograde. Some moments I suspected that I moved backwards as I remained in the same spot. I wondered if I started to run in the opposite direction, would it be possible to escape Bombyonder? Would I really be moving in the opposite direction or would it just appear that way? Could appearances be sufficient? Did I need to consider additional perspectives?

Did I have a perspective?

Is hesitancy a perspective?

Is denial?

I wondered if I looked far enough back, could I erase everything that came after? Could I be a destroyer? Could I have a statue too?

Then I remembered I just killed two men. Me. I destroyed that. On my very own without any assistance. Certainly a destroyer of men, worthy men. But what else could I destroy? Could I destroy an event? A place? A memory? A woman?

Could I find the right balance between creator and destroyer? Could I be both? Could I have it all?

Why not? I was practically a Libertarian.

Instead of "destroyer" couldn't I simply refer to myself as an "eraser"? It sounded less threatening.

I created a grown man using denim, glue, a pencil and a corpse.

Like my reverse Eve blended with Frankenstein's monster.

Maybe that is threatening?

Maybe it's good to be threatening?

When I slipped backwards, I slipped way back to a time when perspective threatened something.

Maybe I wanted to be threatening and maybe I wanted to appear as so?

Maybe I should always try to be so?

Maybe my ticket out of Bombyonder is to be a threat?

Unsigned Note from Yonder

The butter churn dissolves.
Your cue to crank it.
Let me repeat:
the black ring on your finger disappears
when you start producing answers.
There's one way to reach mercy
and it involves a crumbling wall
circling a deepening pit.
I repeat, there are answers
that do not require recollection.
Simply repetition.

Inside-Out Survival

What would it mean to be seen from the inside? Why would anyone want that? I try to imagine what I might be, past the flesh and vessels, deeper than the organs and bones, a microscopic orb that contains a never ending lineage of cruel assbeasts.

Or so I assume. I'm only familiar with two of these generations and that seems a sufficient subject pool. I've heard stories, vague, detailess stories about women and the men who they married.

I suspect it would be pretty terrifying to be able to see that deeply into oneself. For others to see what you spend all your energy camouflaging from yourself. It's never pretty on the inside. Can terrifying be worthwhile? I'm considering worth and its arguments for ways of measurement. Is there worth in the foulness or is foulness worthwhile? I have an impatience with worth, it takes forever to recognize all the while it's here and there, all the places right in front of our faces.

Worth sits there doing nothing making it positively worthless.

Tell don't show, this isn't theatre, these are words, with meanings, these are ideas. Restore, don't omit, we're starving.

After I cut my father's throat, I heard a woman's voice tell me to take what was most repellant and cling it close to my heart, think of it always, love it any way I could manage. That's what it meant to see the inside of him: smoke, blood, animals, monsters, clowns and the long suffering, stifled, womanly advice. When I held that foulness, his foulness, hers, those snakes and worms, that unseemly urge of sex and food. I wished to consume every piece while denying it all and when I embraced that foulness, after all my hesitation, it awoke the orb.

Ignition.

Her voice said that this was worthwhile. Worthwhile to the point of repulsion.

I didn't see it.

I heard it.

Her voice within him, stuffed and suffocating for generations until the oxygen let in by the slit revived her.

How did she get in there? The maternal routed through the paternal? Is that the path to get to her?

Her voice an orb, spinning, warming, burning, drilling.

Was I terrified when I saw what was inside my father?

Most certainly. A gruesome foulness more familiar on the inside than I ever recognized all the times I observed his outside.

My father was full of women. You can't even go to a man to escape. The women are in the men. The women are in the women. Women everywhere women. Invisible. Silent. Shadowy. Vicious. Women.

Could I hold close to my heart the things that came from my father? These woman things in drag? Could I embrace them? Could I make an attempt to love my father for who he really was? Another veil covering the women?

If he's full of women and she's full of women, could I be full of anything else? Can women cancel each other out? What if the opposite of women is simply more women?

What is the sound of one nostril snorting?
Did I have any intention of embracing or loving her?
I wish you could hear the timbre of my snort.
My wineglass-shattering snort.

The Invisible Math That Makes Shit Spin

Confusion around names. To give birth to a child with a different name risks blurred relations. Can this be related? Am I attached to the father and the name I started with? If I change my name, can I change my father? If I have no name, can I be an orphan? These were questions I needed to record.

To give a child a name.

To give a child a name means... who knows what that means.

Something given to children, a gift, a curse... same thing.

Sometimes people combine names to create a new name. A process called confluence. The overwhelming confluence of arithmetic. Orbital arithmetic. Orbular arithmetic? Behind the scenes math. Behind or below? Shadow or dirt? Bomb or BBQ?

All the organic foulness comes with its purpose. That orb that slowed to such a slow spin, barely detectable, at best, lukewarm, I promised myself what I knew I could not accomplish, that I would write and just write and worry later because I'm too critical. I promised what I didn't understand.

So powerful it's Medusa.

Her voice said that men had no idea what's in the hearts of women. Even a quick glimpse would immobilize them. Maybe what petrified them wasn't her gaze or snaked head, maybe what they gazed into was her heart. Something so incomprehensible they couldn't even attribute it correctly. Or perhaps simply feared to do so. It's easier when you don't know your own mind for it is a terrible waste, eggs frying in a skillet for some beast to gobble or create a metaphor to terrorize children.

You can't fry an orb, but you can put it on ice.

You can't fit an orb into a triangle, but you can jam one in.

Triangle as an orbicular dream catcher.

Triangle as a spider full of limitations.

When you have an unwanted triangle: use your own algorithm.

"Voice over voice Medusa" is a variable I named and added myself. I remember that much, this purpose and what eludes me.

Math is hard at work ferreting the heartworms.

Courtship

Terrifyingly Handsome texted saying that he felt attacked by the whole transvaginal probe amendment up for vote in the state senate. The War on Ladyparts was coming for him and Governor Ultrasound was leading the charge. I said I felt the same way and why didn't he come over for some drinks so we could meditate on the politics of uteruses and personal property rights.

He hesitated, but agreed. Because I'm his maker and I made him.

There was an essay on SELF RELIANCE on my coffee table that I wanted to roll up into a tight wand to practice on him. I texted him explicit details.

He took his balmy time getting there. I ascribed his flightiness and irresponsibility to his newness. There was still so much I needed to make him aware of, things I hadn't fully considered when I first got my craft on.

As I waited, I meditated because if I wasn't in control, who was? When he arrived he got right to work on my lifted body, floating all on its own. Thank goodness he remembered to take charge. Learning, albeit slowly. Who knows where I could have floated off to if left to my own devices—or ripples.

He said to hang limply, like I told him to tell me, softly swaying before his very eyes, flaccid and meek like lambs wet-t-shirting it in their blood. I must have overlooked how much in love we were, forgot my great fortune, but it all crystallized as I swung upside down, like an inverted cross not worthy of my savior, a hanged woman held. He told me, in a tone not so different from others, to stop grabbing at his ankles.

I bit his ankle while yelling *YUMBA*.

He shook.

I let go. He flipped me over his shoulder. I panicked, screamed, fearful of the adjustment.

He let me down. In all the ways.

Another time. When I was ready. He would never force me, oh no he wouldn't. His mama raised him better than that.

Why yes, yes I did.

He would take care of all of me so I never had to worry about force again.

"Let me be what you created me for, let me be your relief. Consider me the Blast Wrangler on Yonder. Call me Cow Wrangler of the Crater. Cowboy. Cowhand. Cowman. Let me hear you mooooo, little birdie."

YUMBA!

He said I had a lot of frothy ice in my trunk, made him want to cube and polish it until he smeared himself with puddles. He also said other things that didn't make sense. When I created him I was too general with my specifications and certainly gave him way too much creative freedom. I gave a freedom I never knew, one I'm not sure I cared for. In the end, he said what I wanted to hear, albeit in a creepish way and a bunch of other things I quickly forgot . . . something, something, sure babe, I'll smother her for you, patriarchy, a rose by any other name might be here to distract you from the corpses . . .

I thought that, for I too was once a daughter of the patriarchy. For a moment, I contemplated power and this terror's stupefying reach.

Until we knocked those shitkickers built for one.

Heal me, my corpsed beast. My tasty golem. Show me your glittered heart, heroic bulge, your marked sword. Let me feel it. Pledge it.

It got hot in there.

Like someone turned on the oven to roast a turkey.

And soon it cooled. What was supposed to be frightening wasn't that scary after you got him naked. Maybe I made him too heteronormative: two legs, two arms, one dick, but that's all I could think of wanting. My imagination let me down. I forgot to include the distinguishing features. I forgot horns, scales, tentacles, rusted spikes. Not a single scar! I could have made his eyes glow but instead I made them brown. I could have given him wings or webbed feet, real life super powers. I could have made it so that his anus doubled as an electrical outlet.

Coulda. Woulda. Shoulda.

He bored me.

Yet, I was completely drawn and devoted to him. Call it sentimentality of creation. Call it nostalgia for Um. Call it the flaw of womankind and the only reason the human race continues on.

Call it my cycle of self-abuse.

I never asked him what he called it.

Those days were behind me.

Protection

On discovering my first relic, I'm supposed to contemplate the shield that shields the names and redirects people's attention by way of an unrelated tangent. There's more obviously, because there is still a shield to discuss. I keep dancing around this shield because I don't know how best to use it. I don't believe I know its true purpose but I act like I do because I want to display leadership ability.

I'll show them. It's so circular and shiny I could die. I'll show them they could die.

The shield is protection, the reflection used for its filtered look. That's better than looking directly at the foulness, the power, the ultimate worth straight on, because when looking through reflection, the look becomes a gaze. A gaze is softness and that's where the confusion begins.

We must soften her with something before the smothering, or chewing, or slashing, or whatever we end up doing with her. Perhaps the softness is the smothering. Perhaps the softness is the defense.

In a southern state the man who combined his name with his wife's followed the path investigating workers' rights and recorded the many abuses of the workers. Nobody liked worker abuse, but some were OK with it if they didn't know details and if it meant cheaper prices. People liked cheaper prices so much they made a point of not knowing about it.

I showed my support for the workers too. I signed many online petitions.

I did.

The man frequently investigated reports and rumors while meeting with those he tried to help. Of course those he helped turned on him because every good deed ends in betrayal by those who never asked for the good deed in the first place and prefer you to get the fuck out with your supreme colonial do-good bullshittery. Who shot the sheriff and made this fucker John Wayne?

Well, ma'am, I reckon that'd be me.

The man heard gunshots; ran right towards the gunshots, because he was concerned and brave and don't forget, curious. It's men like that who single-handedly change the world. Right when the world was about to change, that was when the white Dodge hit and killed him. That was when his Wikipedia entry dissolved into dust. Nobody left to update it.

Nobody noticed the boy on the donkey who saw the whole thing. That boy on that donkey who led to the shield. If that boy ever had a Wikipedia entry, it was promptly challenged and marked for deletion.

I considered helping the now dead helping-man's wife, but she never asked and I wasn't one of those people who needed to get mowed down by a Dodge through experience.
Keep moving, no hero to see here.

Let me mosey-the-fuck out.

Back when they married, the helping-man and his wife combined their names to create a new one. Some people considered the name meld to be innovative. Others considered it to be more than a bit unnecessary. Others resented the political implications and possible historical contexts. Maybe they were weird because they liked the attention.

When I was a girl I used to invent my own names. The time I called myself Willow because it was my favorite tree or Sammy Jo because who wouldn't want to swear revenge in a room full of socialites?

Who wouldn't want to be the new Threat Girl?

The newly-named helping-man donated his unwanted work to workers in the southern states and now he's dead, sitting next to me. I made sure to let him know that I knew he was a corpse. I kept pretty strict boundaries with the dead. They unnerved me. They always seemed to know something and call me by my most secret invented names. But not this man. He didn't know a number of things, like what happened to his legacy? What did he do wrong?

Dude, how would I know? I don't even know who you are.

Nobody noticed the boy on the donkey, the boy who witnessed the helping-man's murder was dead too. Did he have a name?

Perhaps, but I didn't know it. He tried to get his mother to recognize his death. She didn't because, well, accepting the death of a child is painful for a mother. I haven't figured out who was the boy on the donkey. He didn't want to leave his mother but he knew he didn't have much time. He showed her his death stamp through a reflection, bright and new from the reflection filter, but it appeared old and faded on his skin. While the reflected vantage looked impressive, it wasn't. That was the memory doing all the impressing.

What did this boy, no longer on his donkey, do aside from witness a vehicular murder? What mark did he make during his brief life?

He drew his mother a picture to help her imagine his death. She refused to look. He yelled, waved his arms, stomped his feet. Still she refused.

Nobody noticed. The mother walked away and ran up several flights of steps. She cried. Didn't she recognize his death? Maybe she did. Maybe that's why she ran. The dead boy followed her up the stairs and saw the extended family of the donkey boy.

This is where it gets confusing. Wasn't the dead boy the donkey boy? Were there two boys associated with donkeys in this historical record? Did the boy become two? One dead, one donkey? It's all so unclear. Did all boys look and feel the same back then? Why donkeys? Where were the bicycles?

Impossible to tell, the details smudged at the seams.

Does it matter?

Probably to somebody.

What I can tell you is that the dead boy asked the donkey boy's extended family to help his mother. He said he tried to leave a shield up against her door so she would understand, but she turned it around.

What exactly did his mother turn around?

The unwanted triangle. She believed in Jesus, not algorithms. Jesus hates numbers.

So do I, usually.

Donkey as the beast of burden. Donkey as an ass. The stubborn donkey. Or was that self-preservation? Smart donkey. Smart Ass. Donkey as a creative force. Evidence that the apostles ate both Jesus and a donkey at the Last Supper. Did the apostles wash the holy meal down with Jesus or donkey blood?

Please provide a viable DNA sample for the footnotes else this entry will be marked for deletion.

The family agreed to help the boy's mother grieve. Or at least see what they could do. The unwanted shield left on the door waited for something to be done. Waiting for something to happen is like slitting your own throat. It's better to have the ability to swallow, even if it hurts. You don't want that foulness dribbling down your fresh shirt. It makes a terrible impression.

The boy on the donkey rides again. Free donkey rides. The confluence of a donkey and a horse is a mule or hinny.

A one-dream donkey. Started with the name, diverged with the boy, and then something well-meaning died. Then came another boy on a donkey. Reborn donkey boy has risen? Younger, more handsome donkey boy brother? Donkey boy 2.0?

He has risen?

Risen from what?

I didn't inquire. He was much too young for me. My attention fixed on Terrifyingly Handsome, my bounded mate.

Names Are Constructs, Not Protection

Not sharing my name only confused The Name Monster. How would he prepare and serve me to its family if it didn't know what I was? When flossing how could it distinguish my flesh from his own teeth? How will he know what to keep to use another day and what to digest and shit out?

The Name Monster didn't realize that certain women kept their names to themselves for protection. If you can't be named, you can't be possessed. Personal armor became modern very early on. Blacksmiths didn't make lady armor. No market they claimed. Would you rather have a peach, My Little Donkey, instead?

Maybe if they tried making armor in different colors. Maybe if they contoured the armor to fit our bodies.

Do we write "shield" with an oval or scalloped script?

As long as it's a flourished script we get to keep it because no man would think it worth taking. The more girly we become, the less valuable our presentation. Our hidden wit allows us to survive and languish.

How do you accessorize your ballistic shield?

With my just-fucking-die-already pumps or if I'm going casual, with my tic-you-to-an-anvil sandals. True style is being beautiful in a way that's as painful as possible. Next time the Name Monster tries to trick me into giving him the name my parents shackled onto me, I will annihilate him with sharpened style straight from Medusa's closet.

Oh, I'll show him my heart, my love—every spike-pitted cranny.

I will petrify him with my own monstrosity. I'll present him a name as limp as the worm I pull from his intestines. I will stomp his tongue flat and make annihilating love on it like a bear skin rug.

Can I do such a thing if I can't even run in those shoes? Can he ever be safe with me around, grinding and sparking all those metal shards?

I wasn't created for safety. On the 7th day an old man took a nap and dreamed of my vulnerability.

Did this man create the Name Monster?

Yes, among others monsters.

What came first, my monstrosity or his?

Yes.

Unsigned Note from Yonder

How fascinating to work in the lone, black-glass office building built in the middle of a cornfield.

How strange to immediately enter the conflict by way of a 19th century French gilt chandelier hanging in the lobby.

How terrifying to be taken hostage again by the same men who slaughtered you the last time they took you hostage.

How handy to use your memories from the last hostage situation to help yourself escape this one by way of the nearby elevator.

How curious to be stopped at the wraith floor and be invited to join the space between life and death.

How tempting the offer becomes once they incentivize you with your very own hand-gnawing kitten.

Recovered Memory

The school district reassigned me to the Kitty Hawk Alternative School. On entering the building they stripped me of my corporeal form. My teacher was a Dragon Lady who glided through closed doors. I followed through walls. She instructed me to call her either Miz Trixie or Duchess Sweetness of the Night Creeps. She was really elderly, like prune-in-a-tanning-bed old. I could tell her intention was to drag me through a long, arduous game of Terror in a Teapot.

I was young, egotistical and considered myself to be much too serious a student for such tactics. My face from those days was what one might call "supple."

I stood before her desk and requested she get straight to the point, what was this terror over me that she possessed? She directed my gaze to a hovering mandala drawn on gold paper. Fancy and swirling, pretty much everything stuffed tightly into a black ring.

I told her, sure, she could pay some guy from Las Vegas $10k to take care of the mandala, but then he'd just come back and ask for $40k and when would it stop? I might have been a wraith, but I could still pick up the paperweight sitting right in front of me and brain her because I was an American and loved the bright crimson sight of freedom.

Violence set me free from what ailed me.

I wasn't afraid to be a patriot because I didn't need grades.

I always depended on the kindness of my father's bombs.

"My dear protégé, you've always depended on what maims you."

Name Monster

1. Lures its prey using a baby in distress to draw victims near the water where it hides.

2. There are numerous penalties for fighting this monster.

3. Should be fought like the monsters from ancient literature, like Grendel's mother.

4. Key to killing this monster is to kill her baby on land, while she's helpless, tied to a tree.

Mandatory Community Service

Like a school teacher educating hoards of young lovelies who didn't know their own loveliness, I pointed out their squalor.

I will be your advocate for five hours a week until I find my bird.

No time to waste coddling these pinked and tanned beauties. They lived surrounded by an inexplicable foulness and they needed to be told of their predicaments.

Just look at your squalor! Look at it!

We rose to recite the Pledge Of Presence alongside the governor and his wife.

"Please like us," the wife urged as she squeezed my hand, "this is our time. We waited so long to be liked and not resented for our success and hard-earned wealth."

We demanded scholarships to which the governor and his wife quickly agreed. Scholarships, a new soda fountain in the teacher's lounge, whatever we wanted, they pledged it as her grip on my hand grew tighter until my fingernail disengaged from its bed. The governor nodded his head so furiously to our requests I felt my neck crackle a little just trying to keep up. Bruises and lacerations decorate the classroom wall. An education delivered in a battered classroom leaves marks.

THE KIND BOMB FELL HERE announced the chalkboard.

The little girl in the front row quoted her grandmother: "Love thy elected official as he loves you."

The governor pledged a revised school lunch plan to include fresh, locally grown produce for any child willing to eat it. He shared his vision for vocational training and community college for any child willing to work for it. If these children would stop complaining and work for what they want, he'll give them the tools. He'll teach them how to fish alright. Just like Jesus.

But don't ask him to love these children when he already had children of his own to love. Specifically he had boys, with his name, who trained to expand and maintain his legacy. He needed to invest his heart into his own legacy, not into charity cases. He had his money to do that work for him.

If the girls would just accept the extra classes and food, show some appreciation, maybe they could break into middle management. Then we could all get along and finally have nice things.

Toleration and commendation! We promised to never desire or request the love or respect of an elected official again. Nor would we expect the love of our of kings and queens, nor the love of our parents or teachers or anyone possessing any status or power over us whatsoever. We would not expect what they did not wish to give because it would be selfish of us to expect things they weren't willing to give us.

THIS IS YOUR TIME TO PROVE YOURSELVES.

For speaking up, the girl in the front row received the honor of the tinsel bomb. She could have kept it, wore it as a pendant, for it was beautiful and showy and would have made her very popular for it was much better than a tiara. They gifted her leverage. She could have used her bomb to advance in the world. She could have developed some ambition and knocked down the competition. She could have used a strategy. She could have grasped the spoils and bought a two bedroom condo in a chic, established part of town.

BETTER LIVING THROUGH OWNERSHIP.

But she was not that kind of girl. She didn't seem to want to make anything of her life. Didn't seem to want nice things or be remembered. A startling and dismal lack of ambition doomed to grow up into a walking human waste collector.

"What I know is what those before me chose to share," said the girl.

She tossed the sparkly grenade right between the governor and his wife. The tinsel swirled, spread around them, exfoliated their flesh, covered their eyes, nose and then the tinsel snaked into their hard, lovely mouths like it a parasite on a pilgrimage.

Sparkle mummies. Glitz-crusted cocoons. Bling wraps.

SPECTACULAR SPA DATE.

Tinsel removes distinction. Tinsel as a beauty solution for the masses. That fifteen minutes of being a flash in the cauldron. Tinsel lures the spiders so the spiders come and spin more tinsel to catch the worms, break them down, make them digestible. Tinsel attracts the eyes. Too much tinsel ruins the tree. Too much tinsel turns into flash.

WARNING: USE TINSEL SPARINGLY.

The girl quoted her grandmother again, "You can dip a turd in tinsel, but it's still a turd."

TOO MUCH TINSEL MAY RUIN CHRISTMAS AND OTHER MILESTONES.

We were OK with tinseled turds. We desired nothing more than their tinsely turdiness.

Have we proved our appreciation for your many gifts?

THANK YOU FOR YOUR BOMBING.

Fluffy Monster

1. A highly-trained creature of evil created to fight evil under the whim of a mighty patriarch.

2. May be adorable, like stuffed-animal adorable.

3. Mildly comical, but not a serious comedian.

4. Inhabits a place where quirky things happen.

5. Known to cover face with cardboard boxes while living inside a slightly larger cardboard box.

6. May have a long giraffe-like neck, like a popular willowy actress.

7. May politely laugh at rape jokes to put men at ease.

8. Known to steal the sphincters of men-at-ease for her personal collection.

Recovered Memory

Once I visited the village of the Goddess and the Astronaut. There were two churches, a bar, a bowling alley and its flea market tables bulged with ping pong paddles and relics. A mostly friendly population that kept to itself. Read about it in *Better Living Thru Time Travel* and always wanted to visit. It seemed to possess that perfect mix of quirkiness and safety. A good weekend getaway. You never know, while in the café sipping an iced latte, you could see a bona fide astronaut order his coffee black. A real explorer who went to the stars and returned to tell about it. An astronaut here to explain how worlds spin and just about anything else you could think to ask.

Except how exactly he became a god in a puffy suit with its own colostomy bag. The world worships what the world worships.

As you probably guessed, the village astronaut was clumsy and boorish when it came to romance or even general conversation. When wooing the Goddess he'd say, "Wanna go for a ride on my rocket, Persephone?"

She'd reply, "My name is Athena and I don't fuck."

Then he'd say, "Wanna see my space helmet? It's in my attic."

Couldn't tell you what the Goddess was about other than she was supposed to be very mysterious and it was extremely important that you never insulted her. Aside from that, all the article described was her stunning beauty, loving gaze and how she transfixed the Astronaut with her "no fucking" policy into a living landmark. Certainly he was under her spell, that she didn't seem to intend to cast, but her existence pretty much obligated her to give attention and time to him. It must have been frustrating to exist as a reference and reflection of something that she didn't care for nor respect.

As gifted as she was, her gift only gave her limited autonomy.

Her gift being full of marvelous goodies for the taking.

Unsigned Letter from Yonder

You will see the church and trees, the gravel road and the graveyard, the altar and the limp snake. You will see my neighborhood as picturesque and you will take a photograph to post on Facebook.

You will receive two pity-likes and your mate will use the opportunity to inject his perceived humorous aside about himself in your comment field.

You will see the death announcement in the softening ice staring back and wonder who put it there.

You will wonder until you are distracted.

You will smell the burnt scriptures and humorless smoke.

You will blow the ashes out your nostrils and wonder how much reached your lungs.

You will wonder did I make all that fire just to kill a snake?

Even if you don't see my matches or smell my accelerants, you will know that I brought the fire.

You will see no flash or gleam in my eyes, you will see I no longer have the strength to carry a torch and you will wonder how I was ever able and what could be incinerated next.

Until you become distracted and forget your new shard of clarity.

    You will forget that you forgot, but I will continue reminding you, we will continue circling you, like maternal buzzards, in plain sight.

Vague Memory

We were sexing it up on a very fine mattress. Experts said sleep would be improved, but sex remains sketchy on memory foam. Sleeping and sexing were pretty much the same for me so I didn't notice much difference. When he poured mouthwash on my chest was that part of the act or the dream? Did he really liken our sex to slitting our throats? That made me think of my father and I didn't want to remember him while I was sexing on a memory foam mattress.

What did it mean that this lover masturbated all over my scarf collection? Was this a trick to keep my neck exposed? Was he serious when he said he wanted to see the latest Johnny Depth film? Was that what reminded me of Heath Ledger in Monster Ball?

Were the hysterics the film's or mine?

Dear Diary,

Servitude to a syphilitic lover is a farce, but the heart wants what sickens it. That's what my father used to say about his marriage with my mother. I never figured out who was the farce and who had the heart. Who had the syphilis? How was it contracted? Did one pass it to the other? Did either ever realize that there was a cure for that?

    Did absence imply rejection? Did neglect imply disgust? I never asked because I needed to eat.

    I was always starving for something.

    My heart beat like a dying whale's sonar, unable to tell the difference between a fish and a torpedo.

    Keep it down, they told me.

    So I did.

Dear TH,

Making out, making excuses, making vegetables for fajitas, making sure the room matches the carpet, making a big deal, making something to eat, making something I know you will like, making chandelier earrings out of telephone wire and cough drops, noises, unidentified squeals, dumb comments, perfecting the corpsed-doll gaze you seem so attracted to, room for ice cream, scam phone calls, a vase holding chained daisies circling a resting bird of prey, conversations seeking eye contact, making fun, making plans, an honest honky joke, brittle pages, a personal withdrawal, why don't you look me in the eye, why don't you?

Things that come to mind after spending the afternoon with you.

Presumably after making love, dowsing the puddles of joint property, I request a conference with the head of your uterined testicles, 3/5 a man, can you honestly say you're a 1/5?

I am in need of a legend to decipher these squiggles.

Why don't you write?

Making a project, fluffy-faced arrangements, a list, the tacos, big scenes and freaking out, making this all up, making it difficult to walk away, a space even smaller, entry-level salary, menacing sounds, making sure you got my numerous messages, progress, salad, making up sprung tales to impress the unimpressable, sense, comparisons, lines, a turn, making another pass, years in the making, making me learn something I already learned.

Making me nervous.

Nervous something will be shown and told, nervous about classes I haven't attended, too close to the bulldozer, having to come up with something on my own, nervous about ultrasounds, slipping deeper into that crater, are you still with me?

Were you ever with me?

Is that something moving inside of you, warming?

Might it be a snake?

Or better yet, a bird?

People standing in the hallway, the disabled, I can't seem to learn it again, need to learn the basics to start a new career, learning the Fourth of July is a lot like Memorial Day, I forgot the many meats, learning of a very negative story for the very first time—again.

Surprised I witnessed it all, yet never wrote any of it down making it unreal.

Getting ready to learn it, will learn to play when I'm older, later I learned she never died but left by choice, by preference, I knew that, wish she was dead, this is getting too personal, watching a video to learn, learning otherwise, how to become stronger, more aggressive, let me use you to my political benefit, stand stoically with your strand of pearls next to me while I publicly confess fucking a golem, more about her, less like her, would really like to get rid of her, why aren't you helping?

Nothing helps.

What was she supposed to do after he bombed her? She had options. She picked what she picked and that was that. My existence made it worse. My weight brought a heaviness that couldn't be expelled, although she certainly tried. If she didn't want me to need her, why did she make me so heavy?

She made what she made. She left what she left which was what she made.

You wouldn't bomb me with your life saving torpedoes, would you?

You would not because I created your torpedoes to be blank. I created you in her blankness, in the blankness of a wanton neglect.

I gave you a blank slate to be the right kind of man and yet you leave it blank.

You must want something more than blankness.

Why aren't you reading my mind?

Or at the very least, my private diary that I write for you.

Don't you want to know me?

XX

Letter from TH

Forgive me, my yondered squaw, I haven't written or visited because I've been making the rounds, surveying the land with its fruits and corpses. There's gold in those pits, I tell you! Your meals cloak the massive diversity of delicacies among these tinseled ruins. I could spend the rest of my life tasting and chewing and shitting. In fact, I just might.

I have no answers to your questions, or at least none that would satisfy, but I do have a question for you. I've met many creatures and beings on my exploits, and forgive me for repeating, but several have insisted that you are a sneak, a snake and a slut. Of course I defended your honor most vigorously and explained you were not a sneak, a snake nor a slut, but a dingbat. I have always been your biggest defender, you know that.

But why would they speak such things? Why were they so very adamant? What actions and words left such an impression on so many? Who were you and are you still her? Please tell.

Your obedient creation,
TH

Recovered Memory

He was a fox. I was a goat. Among other animals. He mentioned FOX News. I said I didn't watch. What a difficult thing to sleep among the howls. The violence of reporting: everything uncovered was under fire, lashing out or blasting. Air strike raining words and teeth. What a horrible thing to qualify for free beasts at every response. What to feed the noise. Feed the fish until they float. Feed the giant wiggle to the whale until it chokes. Feed the dog his instructions. This really wasn't food, it was more like an infection.

    Garbage not fit for throats.

    There was a room that was supposed to be all mine that I shared with him. He left for a day, took his clothes from the closet. I thought he was dead, I hadn't wished for that. After the baby foxes hunted the baby deer and dragged their bodies back to the den, he returned as if he stayed and never left. But he was never really here in the first place. He didn't say where he went or where he got his flashy leather biker jacket that announced CANADA in a semi-intense tone.

    He was so blank, the jacket wore him.

    Sort of like if James Dean, Mickey Rourke and Val Kilmer all took a shit in the same bucket and Judy Chicago, while strung out on meth, sculpted the shit into my lover.

But in more words.
My words.

Recovered Memory

The flood came as massive waves from both directions. We had to crawl to the top, all the way to the attic. This time we couldn't just hang from our fingertips, we had to enter the room and take our fill of airy, lofty ideas. Last time we climbed these stairs, we only took a few scraps of paper when we needed much more. We must have been very young and inexperienced. This time I grabbed the jewelry, something with tangible value I could take to the pawn shop: the too-heavy-to-wear mother of pearl earrings, the thin gold heart and the gem-encrusted bird pin.

Someone said, "hide the bird."

Yes, this time, I hid it. The lizards never knew it was there, even after they read my mind, because I had already forgotten the spot and the desire. To find a new spot, to feel a new desire, you have to forget the old ones. This talent I recently developed.

This talent led the lizards to consider me a minor joke in their roving odyssey.

"Why lookie here, we got ourselves a dingbat."

Perceptions are like shoes and these lizards had none.

If you say so.

"Oh ma'am, you're a dingbat if I ever saw one and I'm looking right at her."

Postcard from TH

Wait a minute, you CREATED me. Does that make you my mother? Did you intend on creating a motherfucker?

Recovered Memory

The unplanned devised a plan to decide what was important and what was unimportant. Passed out the straws and realized they were one short. By luck or accident this was something that happened all unto itself. Perhaps it was a pregnant plan performing atrocities from bed.

It was about taking a stand.

And about shoes. I lost mine, then stepped on something sharp. On this hill even the grass was sharp and cracked.

Did I bleed?

Did it matter?

Dyeable shoes making do in a shit economy. Drab shoes. Sample shoes. Seasonal. Heeled. Sparkled. Sneaks. Tying on the discounted. Discounts for the hoard. You couldn't discount how his political process creeped out his guests but nobody wants to be rude to the guy providing the dinner and booze. They all decided to keep things light. This is what they agreed. They will not think about pictures of his penis neither angry nor sated.

What penis?

No penis to see here.

Exactly.

The pregnant carried weight. The pregnant had to go. Wobbly never won a beauty pageant.

Out-of-sight and off the scale.

A cart full of discounts and grimaces making way to higher ground. Maybe there was a flood coming or maybe I was there for the view or maybe I was taking my stand at a very reasonable price, albeit one with blisters.

Dear Diary,

Bully incense, bully shake, bully back, drunk by bullying, bully for me.

What a bully, what an ending she's gonna get, what desserts I'm preparing for her.

Running the store, learning more about the woman behind the register, like reviewing a biography page and knowing there's nothing else to know, the social pressure to stop and listen to an opposing viewpoint is oppressive. Salt piled eyes, an exquisite jump rope made of salt, no salt for lunch, shake her, the station shakes, operational shakes, shakes and yells, crafted, hand shaken and twisted, shake that thing, shake it like a broomstick.

Maternal disorder brining in the oven.

There was a foulness that I didn't know what to do with. It didn't go away, so I named it Lily, put a sweater on it, locked it in a box and put it in another box full of other random stuff I didn't want to review. I knew I was supposed to look after it, walk it around the block, let it get some fresh air, feed it, but I never did that because it was very foul and I hated looking at it. Not only did I hate looking at it, but I hated thinking about it so I tried very hard not to think about it. But Lily's box in a junk box kept appearing in the most precarious places—in the bath, in bed, in surgery and eventually the tattoo parlor where she made her break.

Back then I didn't want the tattoo, but I didn't feel like I had much of a choice, I didn't want to challenge Mother. I needed my job. I wanted to continue existing so I accepted her mark and she allowed me to continue since I was no longer a threat. The tattoo was vulgar and I didn't like that either, but I figured now that I was older my appearance didn't matter so much. The point of this memory was that foulness spreads, like the tattoo that started at my ankle and soon crawled up my thigh like a dandelion vine.

Father might have called it "brand recognition" or "platform building."

As my brand spread it became less foul, more tribal and leopard-like, Lily Munster-like and damn, that's one sexy vampire and the voice of reason in a house of monsters. As I examined my thigh closer I remembered half a lifetime ago when I was a monster without reason with a mullet, permanent wave and anklet.

We're not magnets, two like-monsters don't cancel each other out. Or we are magnets, repulsive to our sameness?

I'm not allowed to ask.

I'm not supposed to live with questions but without, leave them to fend for themselves in a box in a box, muffled.

Text from Lily

LilyInABox: You lost our blue-headed orphan already? WTF ? ? ?
When I get out of this box I'm going to chew out your asshole like it's Bubblicious.
xoxoxo

Home Cooking

There were many things she could have done, but the first thing Mother did was serve me take-out spaghetti on a cracked glass plate. I noticed the small worm first, then the large bloodworm that looked a lot more like a flaccid penis than an invertebrate. Blood dripped onto the floor as I wrapped the worm in a napkin and carried it over to the toilet to flush.

I told you I was a vegan.

I wasn't a vegan, but fuck her with her fleshy noodles.

So like her to never cook anything herself, as generations before, subsisting on their cheap convenience. Not like she ever ate a worm. She wouldn't deign to eat a worm. She who protected who she hated. She who punished her protectors. She who poisoned those who loved her. Well, I'm not afraid of her hate.

Then the hostile takeover of her uterus happened. She might have forgotten to take the poison bomb. She might have forgotten to bring a map. I think I forgot the spot when it happened.

She never forgot the spot. She claimed it a long time ago. She built that. She claimed she could chain me to a post and make me stay there until I mummified or she could take it all away leaving me as dust. Sometimes she threatened both. Sometimes it seemed threat creation was her only pleasure.

Wearing a bright red dress and leaning on a crutch, she said the worms were to treat my sickness and multiple mental illnesses. Unknowingly, I wore mirror face and saw my reflection in the cracks. I threw the plate with the noodles at her but hit a different woman instead.

Damn that hurt and that was what I feared.

The negligible punished for the purpose of having purpose, their crack-given meanings. I gave that dingbat a meaning then hid in my room, locked myself behind two layers of doors. Checked my messages.

No word from Terrifyingly Handsome.

I needed something to talk to and a corpse would do nicely. Just that morning I drew the Tower. Everyone knows that the best advice when dealing with the Tower is to remain calm and not react.

Creating scenario action plans only limits your possibilities.

There's never been a tower that I didn't react to and this time was the same as all the others.

I set something, not saying what, on fire.

Reactions have consequences and consequences are the new order. Consequences are results.

Obviously.

This experience inspired me to become a chef. After the fire, I invented a new open-flame cooking style and published a cookbook called *12 Dishes that Rhyme with Medusa*.

Text from Lily

LilyInABox: Hello, anyone there? What did you do with that orb? Damn, dingbat, it's like somebody popped that bubble-gummed brain of yours. Anything left?

Dear Lily,

Pondering what I will tell the worms when they ask who they're feeding on. Anyone can pronounce a name with enough time and practice.

This name echoes, incessantly, taunting.

But one cannot live off of a name.

Names have no meat, only bones. This name is not my representative and will not sate the worms. Contrary to popular opinion, swallowing the worm at the bottom of the swamp will not make you a man or give you his powers.

Contrary to popular opinion worms cannot be sated.

XX

Diary on Healthy Living

Advice about food from those who prefer not to eat, noodles in bulk, good value, advice about placement and presentation from those who don't look, use more senses, taste is not an option, to remain calm and not react, competitions are the systems that keep us in check or in massive cardboard checks, long signatures overflowing short lines, contesting what you're served may insult the server.

Never insult the person handling the food.

To meet the challenge, be low key and off the radar, become a woodworker, sell large substantial things, sell small things to people who won't buy the large things but feel guilted to buy something, little things add up, big doesn't sell everyday, get up and approach people, in person, use a phone, advice on bicycles, go to the casino, move to the mountains, cut the skin behind the fin, run between their legs in such a way as you won't get trampled.

The cameras in her eyes don't hide what's happened to the food, they don't record it either.

If money is a hurdle in your relationship, write off the money to charity, find a patron to finance your love, steal from a pig's belly.

I don't feel qualified for health, I find it difficult, elusive to the taste. Illness and its distinct flavor makes a memory, sour and bitter and covered in cream.

Only someone thin should ever try something so substantial and caloric.

Don't download that app, you don't know where it came from, you don't know how much time you'll spend using it, it'll zap you, rob you of your life, make you sick, make you want what it shows you and hunger for cash.

Don't compare cooking, or salary.

Never leave a wet spot.

Never drink from the swamp.

Never order off the menu.

The menu lies.

The presentation exploits.

Recovered Memory

We were honored to be placed at a large table with Milton Berle, his green eyes matched his mangled pea tie in a very monied style. Rich. Mesmerizing. This was the Golden Age of Eating. Milton Berle didn't chew his dinner, he chomped at our tits. He almost suffocated in our overflowing bosoms. We watched his face turn blue, then back to gray.

He asked if we did anything other than sit around watching our titties sag. He asked where he might find our names listed. He asked if we produced anything even slightly resembling tangible results.

We watched his eyes turn a milky black.

He looked at me and asked about the progress on the legacy project. I told him I was occupied sexing my corpse golem. I told him my intention to repair a motherfucker. The way to a man's heart is to serve him his stomach.

Milton wasn't impressed. There are no legacies for golems. I put all my eggs in a corpse like a dingbat. He choked on his soup and blamed me. He said I'd choke too and it would be my fault because I never listened or respected tradition. He called me one demented slut before falling asleep in his chair.

This resulted in him missing my toast where I joked about the many shifting names. One day Milton, *Who Wants to Marry a Millionaire* the next.

Maybe if he had stayed awake, he would have been impressed with my wit.

Once I thought I wanted to marry a millionaire. My big white gown attracted all kinds of attention that I didn't intend, like being a reality TV celebrity without the competition. Back then I thought I was on my way to someplace where I could have a life of my own making.

But just because I wasn't competing didn't mean it wasn't a competition.

Some other bride won the groom's hand. How did this guy earn his status as prize in the first place? What were his goodies? He convinced everyone he was an old woman, so hunched and wise, we found value in his advice and believed whatever he told us. For instance, men aren't the only things that are recyclable, personas could be recycled too. He showed us how we could dye all these gowns and shoes to wear again for a fancy ball or the avant-garde Druid funeral scheduled to reveal itself in its due time.

If I could have married that guy, I would have been ready for anything.

Dear Diary,

Frankly the human buffet served to the worms just isn't cutting it, worms moaning that every limb and organ taste like dirt, the rhyme, reason and order of waiters matter and there wasn't any of that in this spread.

Wilted beets, limp cucumber, celery with the biggest veins you've ever seen, talk about one harsh salad, tuna, puma, barracuda, something something pupa, work with what you got, make what you got work.

Fishing for the magic egg that hatched, the one with the flower on top, the one that contains the habitat, there's lettuce leaves to chop, you're going to need to go up a size if you want space for a birdcage, you're going to have to piece back the shell.

You're going to need to go through the tubes and packages of individually wrapped birds, you need to be efficient, you need to be an aggressive virgin of stones, I am focused on arrangement, I offer an anti-linear historical outline to anyone receptive to a spiral web, I'm offering an offer I can't explain.

An arrangement to feed the dog, a dried rose arrangement that smells like an orchid's vagina, some arrangements create jealously, others distrust, others a temporary lover, like a temporary uncle long divorced away to a place where he's no longer your uncle and doesn't send birthday gifts.

Seating arrangements and their destiny-making powers.

Find the biggest assbeast and seat me at his table, these worms need to eat.

12 Dishes that Rhyme with Medusa: **Table of Contents**

Appetizers
Guava Dragon-breath Salsa
Sliced Barracuda on Melba
Alpha Alligator Cola Puffs
Whale Enema Matzo Ball Soup
Oujia in a Blanket

Side Dishes
Missing Wolf Okra
Roasted Worm Raga

Entrees
Kafka Penis-Noodle Saga
Fried Cheetah Lingua
Spider Nausea Flambé

Desserts
Baked Apple Troika
Vodka Orange-Glazed Hydra

Dear Diary,

Something about choices, some kind of lesson and I'm just not interested in learning more, wanting to go back to default settings, wearing a power tie around my waist and wondering who died, wearing a teal dress no one would ever remember, why should I care about being remembered, looking for an instructor who thinks I'm enough, wondering about murder via pillow and its success rate.

Nancy Drew and the Case of the Feathered Esophagus

Wondering about generational difference, what difference, wondering about the cultish, is there any respect to be found and what brand should I purchase, wondering what's private and why, show me your hoohaw like you just got engaged, wonder how much this is all going to cost, another body added to the count, no need to wonder why she thought this spot, it's ugly and dank and totally her, wonder why they're so afraid, where's this nervous laugh emanating from, this spot lacks hilarity, wonder what they'll offer, like they have something to offer, like they ever bring anything for me.

This spot takes people to their bodies, must have come to this place by choice, whose choice, what choice, there is no choice, this spot is turning into a real dumping ground, this spot and its new owner and I'm going to suggest that they offer to hang our coats when we arrive because the last time it was a stampede.

I'm going to suggest that they act like they want us here.

I'm going to suggest an extreme makeover.

I recognize this spot, its mustached rounder, its feathered triangle, argumentative squares.

Knew this foul spot, I've known it, I knew it.

Eating sour cream & onion chips while walking into the huge maze of spot and wishing it was Funyuns, this spot and its hippie Whole Foods vibe, this spot and the tainted breaths I bring to it.

A little barren and scary, you never heard of this spot, go downstairs and check it out, check your purse, deposited a few cents so this check doesn't bounce, they recommended cash so I wrote a check, check your GPS, check your invitation, check your FB account for something about a workers' rights bill, be sure to like it so people know you care, check on the bedroom, check out this boutique, check the iron, get your check-up, you can drop that check in the mail any day now.

Checked all the choices, checked for chalk lines, for ash, for anything charred, for anything organic, I checked this spot hard.

Checking out while checking it out.

More About the Bombing

Some were shot. We considered them lucky because the bullets were really small. They could barely feel their pin-prickled deaths. Over before they knew it and soon back to their daily routines. For them, nothing much came up, a random glimpse of a favored childhood toy, breakfast cereal, a glass of Tang, all forgettable, pleasant, tame, nostalgia's prime material.

The rest of us endured our deaths for years. It took a long time to be crushed by a falling sky and even longer to be smothered by it. You could barely feel the weight holding you down. Each gasp full of thin air and feathers, practically tickled. Our daily dying became our infinite routine. We became so well acquainted with it, we could do it in our sleep, squirming, crying for it to stop, squeezed like hotdogs, choking on feathers.

It never stopped and we barely died, just felt the dying continually. The more we recovered, the more it killed us, over and over until we couldn't forget a damn thing. I couldn't forget the penises, so many angry penises. Pissed penises squinting. Marching penises of fury, poised to take back what's rightfully theirs.

Oh ee oh, ohhhh!

The Pencil Dick Dilemma and its Unlikely Collaborations: A Play in Infinite Acts

Blob Monster

1. Often hangs his dick outside his pants for attention.

2. Jokes about hanging his dick outside his pants.

3. Screams when he doesn't receive attention.

4. Screams can be shrill and piercing.

5. Sometimes goes by the m.o. "Big Tiny."

Dear TH,

You don't bring me gift baskets, you don't carve me apples, you hardly text. I remember when we used to sex on a mattress built on vaguely reconstructed memories. I only meant to create a destiny of my very own, unmarred by co-pilots. I never bombed anything. Except myself. I don't deserve such accusations.

    Perhaps the mystery of the flooded basement laboratory might better explain our awkward encounters, the War and its AWOLed heroes, tufts of hair grown over the bullet holes in their backs, tufts like kudzu, the stolen donkey rode to the shipyard and off to America to breed. Doom is the new sexy, my love. The legacy of KFCs in this area doomed to repeat itself. How our health now suffers for what we didn't know then and won't acknowledge now. How we filled our bellies with poisoned love. Battered, deep-fried bombs of doom placed so gently in your mouth.

    Things water for you to swallow.

    There used to be a movie theater in front of this house. Now there's a bigger theater in front of some other spot. What does it mean to give someone the black face? I'm afraid that's all I can offer and it's so very little and why can't that be enough for you? Would you be less appalled if I called it blank face? Standoffish belligerence in blank form which is not the same as free form but often confused to be interchangeable. I've done this before, it ends badly for me. Blank, black, blaring, blubbering.

When in doubt, don't. Just don't. Stay with what you know.

You know me.

Really, you do. Look inside yourself, it's me you'll find.

It's the intention, not the results, you wish to immortalize. Trust me, your memories are recovered holy myths, at best. Intentions always purer than results. What does it mean to be a total pale face?

It's the best.

No, it's nothing, barely there, just a reaction waiting until the tongue swelling goes down. Waiting for everyone to forget and get back to eating. When you warn of a person's intention it calls out the warriors on horseback. It's being defensive. I'm feeling defensive and hoped you'd be on my side. I intended a go-to guy. We put on our clown faces to welcome our violent allies into our bowels. Or bombs. Maybe we're cannibals after all. I laugh with you so you can laugh at me. Results tell us to avoid needles. Results tell us sandals are better for walking than coffins. Why am I in such a rush to get to the end when I feel like that's the last place you'll be?

To avoid meeting the historical figures with the pieces to this result. The killers and the killers of killers. Results told us a priestess is never better than her goddess. Intention wanted her head. Intention wanted her fed so she could keep ailing. Darling, I suffer from perpetual nausea and the more I choke up, the worse it gets. Won't you at least hold my hair?

Would a background check help explain any of it? There is no background. You have no background except my own which isn't yours and doesn't fit the results. I don't inhabit the results. I inhabit you.

Born with Medusa face and given petrified aspirations, I wasn't allowed to use the big knife in the kitchen else I might have cut out my heart. Or cut someone's throat. They knew I was dangerous, but never told me. I wasn't even allowed to cross the street. Instead beheaded and turned invisible. Any generosity gristled for the stones, a barren rock garden that bloomed granite and empty gazes.

But what I could kill wasn't what made me the danger I am today. My danger is what I can create out of trash and rubble and thrift shop bargains. My results make me more dangerous as a maker, homemaker, bed maker, meal maker, man maker, bird maker.

My darling, you are the result. My lovely result seeping with my intentions.

Are you frightened that your penis keeps ending up in my spaghetti? Would you be insulted if I scraped it off to the side? Does my gaze not fulfill all your worldly desires? Why did I bother creating you with desire in the first place?

Because it was my desire.

Will I see you at the One Million Angry Penis March?

XX

Letter from a Lover, Possibly a Son

How can I write when I have nothing but your mandatory blankness? I do want something more than blankness, but I'm afraid it's not what you want. I'm only blank because you won't allow me to fill myself with my own self. You leave me in limbo. Your limbo. Not mine. How cruel, like a snake almost swallowing its prey. When it comes to answers you bloviate like a lizard fart.

You are not something that can fill me.

I'm afraid I don't follow your disjointed narrative, this narrative that offers no place for me. I fear these implications of my assigned role in your historical revisionism. Consider me uncompelled. I'm afraid my penis will dissolve with your disapproval. I'm an object fearful of my purpose. Am I to be your lover-cum-son or your fleshy blow-up doll? Do you fantasize about sticking objects into my bullet holes? I'm afraid to say that your cooking terrifies me. What punishment follows that admission? You create terrible meals no person should ever have to eat yet you keep boiling and frying and baking monstrosities and expect me to fill myself. When I swallow your victuals, I feel like I'm swallowing my siblings and countless other victims.

I'm afraid I will never love you. I'm afraid I might not even like you. I'm afraid I absolutely, positively despise your very essence. Please, let's not force this.

You have no business publishing cookbooks.

TH

Spot Monster

1. If you like it, stick a flag in it.

2. If you don't, tell it to get out and be damned that you did.

Letter from Lily

Check for the hat that feels like a joke threatened by an algorithm that doesn't obey order. You don't have to find it funny, you just have to find the one that fits your reason.

It's a risk putting on a straw hat. It could catch on fire. Do you have an infestation of snakes that needs to be addressed?

You can store a lot of blue juice in a ten-gallon inner tube but that assumes you're thirsty. Can you make sense of the dryness of your tongue? Is it what you can swallow?

Pink hats are for lizards. Do you have the scales?

A visor might do what you want, but will it do what is required? Will it cover your crown? Will it cover what entertains the monsters?

A strong wind holds no shape, hold on to your botched bonnet.

Truly,
Lily

Dear Diary,

Disintegrating pillow cover exposes a disintegrating condom wrapper, glass cutting through from the inside reveals a hole, lots of pillows, rows of cushions, lamp for sale, dirty pillows straight from mother's tit, edible like pillows, money on the pillow, covering my front and back with pillows, pillows in cases, just in case.

What's this going to cost?

There's always a price for thoughts, a price for asking the question, a price to get the answer.

A small gun nestling in the pillow dreams a warm dream of transcendence, shameful urges as bullets rattle "no such thing." Just more holes to be bored.

Biting through the pillow, water pillow down, wanting my pillow, a washed pillowcase makes a fresh start, pillow in the overhead, resting corpse on the pillow, so many stains.

Did anyone notice the pillow?

All glass front door and its deadly knobs, washing wine glasses in a shark-filled sink, careful, something is delicate, glass ceiling partially open, ambitious balloons float on through and never look back, or maybe it's a trick, cramming cereal, milk and glass into a disposal that's simply had enough, suicidal motors.

How can I blow through these windows?
Can I bore through?

Hair dryers like glasses, wearing glasses the whole time, waking through a glass window is different than crashing through a ceiling, blue like liquid glass, breaking the glass, knocking the wine, fumbling with birth control, caterpillar-like creature on a branch eating holes in leaves, spilling the red kool-aid all over history, spilling under the bed, leaving out the pill, a pill to change his aura, Phil Collins making a comeback going down on a monkey, wised up that instinct makes a good beat, pills in the night light, pills in the mist, pills in the belfry ringing for a glass of water, pills in the wrong coats acting suspicious, the pills can't sleep and ask for a glass of milk, unpronounceable pills and their ingredients who inhabit the urine, forgetting the pills, the man behind the pill, stay clean.

Remembering the glass in the pillow and the woman who swallowed it all.

The Pill Book: The Personal Observations and Musings of a Fractured Matron as a Historical Document

Unrecovered Memories

I can't remember if she ate my heart or squeezed it for veins.

Did the worms eat my heart?

Or did my squeezed heart burst worms?

I can't remember what I wasn't supposed to speak.

I can't remember if she screamed when she saw my blood or laughed when I screamed at the sight of my blood.

Or did I scream at the sight of worms?

I can't remember if she was my mother on my mother's side or my mother on my monster's.

I can't remember if the nightmares gave the results promised.

Who recorded memories?

Was it the sensations they wanted noted?

I can't remember what leaked and what was trapped.

I can't remember the horizontal.

I can't remember the stingers but I do remember wanting to use them to hurt someone.

I can't remember who wrote "All roads diverge from Medusa's head."

I can't remember getting these snakes hot-glued to my scalp but I remember the itching.

Moth Monster

1. Often wears bright red dresses to trick its victims into "seeing red."

2. Sometimes known as Mothra. Other times known as the Mummy.

3. To overcome this figure of JUSTICE you must symbolically destroy both the worms and the bombs.

4. This means eliminating the perception of opposites.

5. This means eliminating the perception of union and/or balance.

6. Yin and yang: a joke played on invaders and capitalists to distract them from recognizing the GRAND SHATTERED MOSAIC.

Dear Diary,

The beginning of something marks an ending of something else, the end is The Lovers, the future is The Lovers, the future over the hump and into the swamp, the future an implosion-happy bridegroom, the future is the casino paying out poorly printed money, it's going to hurt, foul future strung, looking back at you.

    An advertisement stuck on my Ace of Spades, an advertisement printed underneath the advertisement on my Ace of Spades, the future is bifocals, ads on a deck I already paid for, ads on a deck I shoplifted long before advertising was invented.

    It's complicated, it's counterclockwise, it skips around.

    These cards portray the children of snakes, my second favorite deck portrays the parents of propaganda, how is my baby being telecast, how does my baby have more market share than me?

    I consider the reversed, understand nuances, understand it doesn't change much, four piles of cards implicating the same destiny, the Adorable Puppy used to be something else, something vicious, now he's just playful destruction, now when you hit him with a rolled up newspaper he bites your lip while making enthusiastic love to the cavern of your neck.

Somewhere there's a sincere young man mumbling, "that's really beautiful," on a YouTube video.

Going back in time to teach primitive women how to assert themselves.

Might that be dangerous?

Someone has to do it, the lover's head among the fancy spread with meats and champagne, things change to paper dragons, things change like a mighty empire, things change with the Lover wearing an insensitive mask, yes, it's good when they teach ladies how to wrestle.

There's a fast-food restaurant called SPERM where the willow tree used to be, but one question, what's on the menu? There bald men read your future by gazing into your toilet.

The bald man looking through my bowels picks the High Priestess, he fishes the signifier out of the bowl, these cards are showing their wear, this card stuck on the back of my underwear, the King and Queen of Diamonds tumble out, the face of the Magician worn off, wishing that mage met the Empress and felt something close to abundance.

There's a spunky sperm who was never allowed, a sneaky seed quite sure his mother would have loved him if she bothered to let him fertilize and get to know him.

The spunky sperm wants to be seen, he wants people to notice him, don't mind him, he just wants attention, everything he does is for attention.

This admission makes a difficult time shuffling the waterlogged deck.

I don't need clubs, I need a pair a pants, can't show up in only underwear, people expect decency, people expect a cover up, people expect someone to wear the pants around here, people expect the imaginary to know its place and not sneak into the imagination until its invited.

The boy cut his neck on a hookah while fleeing on a donkey and now his mother and father are here to claim him.

Why should I cooperate?

Because we must do something to pass this time along to the next in line.

The 3 of swords can tell you if you're compatible or not.

The attic doesn't exist, it stands for something unreachable by gut.

She's wearing the red dress rippling in my reflection, I flush a thousand times, flush as hard as I can.

She remains red and rippling.

That is what the Tower card warned about and this is how I failed that advice.

How can there still be water to fill the tank?

How am I so unloved?

The meaning of the Devil is passion and temptation, it's not the passions or the temptations that are foul, it's the people who own them.

Foul unlovable people.

There is no Hate card, I smudge what is before me on the stall, in the deepest red and brown, far far past hate, post-post-hate.

The Dragon Strikes, a Recovered Memory

When the dragon first came, it was paper that shredded easily in my hands. When the dragon returned as a beast of parachute pants, I needed a blade to deconstruct it. Unclear what its next incarnation would be, but I knew it would return stronger and I'd need a better weapon.

The city still stood in the water contemplating whether to repair and rebuild or to abandon itself for a safer space more inland, away from rising tides and regenerating dragons. It's a dangerous thing to pull down the waterlogged walls and to pull up the mildewed carpet. Every layer hides a bundled corpse that stinks and won't stop rotting no matter how nicely you ask.

It's a dangerous thing to wait around for a dragon's return but it might be more dangerous to try to run from it. If the dragon wanted a brain, there was a mostly fresh one hooked up to a machine in the attic, exposed, without even a sheet covering it. If the dragon wanted a different brain, there were several floating down the avenue, unclaimed.

I had real options. I could have dressed like a dragon and picked a fight with a wolf.

Or I could have played dead.

Dear TH,

These days my fantasies involve pillow fights and black and white films. Let's try again. Maybe you'd be happier without a penis? No more motherfucking! Maybe you could be my sassy eunuch friend? I can revise you. I can fix everything that's wrong, my beloved corpse project, with a few minor edits. Let me delete your teenage angst and tweak these confused desires.

    Let me make you right.

XX

Vacation from the Bombing

We were away for a song, vacationing in a hamper built to confuse until ferrets weaseled their way between the sheets. It became an unwashed wilderness full of prying betrayals. The ferrets took shits like other mammals took breaths. Then the laundry arrived in a big bag named Stagecoach to bring us back home.

    We didn't want to go back home. We didn't want to continue this vacation either. We didn't know what we wanted or who we were or what we were supposed to be doing. What we knew was our resentment. We resented it all and we wanted out.

    Even if we weren't quite sure what it all was or what was out there.

    "When will the aristocrats be arriving?" the coachman kept asking. The coachman's life purpose revolved around aristocrats and my existence prevented their return and that was fine by me because of resentment.

    The aristocrats may return when they have happiness to share. When they're interviewing managerial candidates from the disinfected, washboarded gallows who've been rowing this

Bombyonder in place. When the mansion's library has more than two shelves of books. When a spine is cracked. When an ear is dogged in a way fitting for a page. When the publishing wealth comes marching in. When beggars rip off the aristocrats fine threads, forcing them to prance for stained panties. When someone finally claims this platinum penis for once and for all.

Or is it a sterling tampon?

It fits so simply in my unread palm. This plug is my power. I grasp for its weight without curiosity of its application.

Curiosity killed the spot.

A bomb for your thoughts.

A bomb to let it all hang out.

These are the days of the War on Spots.

Have I bombed in this mysterious miniseries?

Cancellation after cancellation. Online petition after petition. The sequels never end.

"Your Twitter campaign is powerless against our well-oiled masters," they laughed all the way to their candy-coated vaults.

A Newly Discovered Mystery

Kids from a local high school were mysteriously dying. Nobody trusted those kids and then boomba, dead! We would have blamed those kids if they were available to blame but their murders left no choice but to dig elsewhere. Letters found implicating an alien-feminine tree were missing the necessary maps and directories. Somebody's lover recorded events for posterity or maybe historical integrity. Somebody's father directed. A lizard perched on a bookshelf to observe the events. Nobody agreed so each established their own versions and carried on as if that's how it happened.

That's how it happened.

When I arrived to observe the wedding, I hoped to identify the murderer by his behavior while noting numerous dreadful people who deserved equal punishment. All the signs and banners, tiny green snakes with brown spots entwining themselves on any finger that could grip. Something preyed on ignorance. Such easy pickings. Trouble. Lines. Trouble and passage. Those few hours didn't explain murder or lifetime commitments.

No explanation needed. Someone turned.

Turned out the mothers were the murderers. For a variety of accomplished reasons accomplishing somebody's intentions.

Or desires?

Nobody could name a single desire. It was all very vague and untantalizing. Cold fried chicken served at a wedding?

Everyone ate it right up.

Letter from TH

I sense you expect a certain kind of gesture from me although what possible gesture I could not possibly imagine.

Princess of Parody, desire never crosses my mind, you want to cut me and I don't even know your name.

Not even your stripper name.

How can I trust what I cannot name?

How can I know what I cannot fathom?

Who are you to expect such loyalty while remaining nameless?

I never asked for a maker. I never asked to be made. I never agreed to you. At first I tolerated you because you were all I knew, but you made an independent, self-reliant man, you told me to go out and make my mark. So I went out and met others, your betters, kind and generous, the kind of people who don't slash and shoot, the kind of people who don't build bang-bods to make themselves feel whole. The people I met told me all about you.

Dear Tycoon of Tyranny, my sources claim that you're a lost succubus here to fuck out my soul. A man-making parasite who eats her prey when she's used them up. Is that the intention or the mystery? It would explain your troublesome questions.

Your meaningless, emotional statements. The bite marks on my shoulders. The zip ties adoring your shoe rack.

How can I be expected to maintain a correspondence with colonial building violence wrapped in obscurity and hysteria? Why are you obsessed with pointless mystery or intention? There is no mystery. Only my penis. The intention of the shrill disorder lacking a tangible goal. Nobody cares enough to read to the end of your veering psychotic break.

I am not your prince. I am not your literary puzzle of love. I am not your mutli-layered adventure of lust and doom. I am not your hairy-legged French maid. It's all an invention in your mind. Your silly, prince-crazed mind. Don't you know, women don't need princes anymore. You created a human being to treat as a toy as an alternative to psychiatric treatment that you very much need. You fling words like shit and smear your intention on the walls hoping someone will mistake it for art.

I will not make that mistake.

I am my own being out of your control. My sources assert that I am a swan of grace full of a sophisticated gray light created to be part of a significant legacy. I'm special like that. You are heavy like a fish-filled whale and weigh me down. I need to fly. While you may have created me, you did not earn me, I am not your possession. How many ways can I say it.

NO, YOU MAY NOT REVISE MY PENIS.

What I mean is that you gave me life, of sorts, and that's where what you have to offer me ended. Please don't contact me again.

TH

Dear TH,

The bomb as epidural to numb below with a side effect of causing concern throughout oneness with a true generic. The bomb as a block buster. Disconnect as release from connection, the severing of familial spinal cords, to no longer represent, to no longer stand in for the assigned. To be one without a brand is to be one without a name and distinct from tribe. I have no platform to stand on, no banner to drape a man's corpse in, no goal or plan.

    Yet I have created you, in an image I created, you are all the sums of my vision, whether I foresaw the results or not.

    You are not an exception even though we all wish to be unique, don't we?

    You are generic, something created using existing materials and form, based on a long-existing idea, devised by a no-name brand. You're an image treaded and grooved from existing images. A morphine & roofie cocktail I drank to wash the taste of vomit out of my mouth. I drank you and shriveled and knew not why I couldn't sleep. For that, I am sorry. I should have known better. Intention loses its value after it seeks a brand.

    You are the cheapest of your category created to distract and generate a dull malaise. You are a son of a snake, son of a sneak, son of a slut.

Snakefucker.
Sneakfucker.
Slutfucker.

Yet I still believe it both valuable and possible for your generic experience to contribute to the fold, to aid in reaching new destinations not yet imagined, preferably destinations suitable for birthing birds. I have yet to meet a man willing to entertain the birthing of birds. Yet men want feathers for their pillows and comforters, eggs for their omelets, beaks to chew their food for them. Some man must eventually conclude that you cannot have a telephone without a system, hanging along with gravity in a whole variety of ways. The block is so obscured it leaks into absolute novelty. Your lack of vision infuriates me. I gave you so much more to utilize, yet you don't even try.

You cannot have love without the post office. You cannot have love without the notion of a substance. You cannot have love with only a single bang. You cannot be a lover without intention. Those without a womb spurt a lot of jizz.

I failed because I didn't hot glue what mattered. I failed because you're a knock-off corpse sewn together in a bombshop. An imitation of flesh rot, imitation meat product.

What was I thinking?

It's difficult to think when one is alone barraged by her voices. When you were with me, you kept those voices away, my scarecrow. Now they return.

The block is an open question widened by the bomb. This block and its pressing situation is empty of agony. You cannot make love to a pressing situation, there is no opening and nothing jumps. While blocking the experience one should only be blocking the experience by being completely aware that the experience is blocked. I can't hear you, my fingers plug my ears, but I see you and you are dulled to a gruesome level of egocentricity. You and your pretentious, refurbished penis, how laughable.

I am being completely generic and vulnerable to the point of infringement. Your existence can only exist connected to my existence. You cannot takeover and you cannot flee outside my bombed boundaries.

You cannot have love with a serious business decision. You collective cog, you banal snap and edge, you paradox of restraint, you horrible splattered gossip of vital information blowing like a rib cage through another rib cage hurting like a cracked rib, caged.

Return and repent. We can make this work.

Sincerely,

Scarlett St. Agnes
(my stripper name: first pet, childhood street name, all you had to do was ask)

Recovered Memory

As the unnamed mother's pregnancy progressed, it became obvious that what grew inside her was not a human fetus. Sadly for her she was guarded by an imposing dragon that prevented her rescue. No matter what we tried, we could not penetrate the dragon's simple wagon-forted body defense surrounding our unnamed mother. Terribly possessive, the dragon used her unlimited resources of flames and carbon monoxide to quash every valiant attempt.

Soon we realized it was too late for the unnamed mother even if by some grace of mermaid she could be reached. All we could do was close our eyes, sit back and listen to her scream wretched descriptions of how her body contorted.

"My spine is a spiral staircase! The agony!"

"My toes are helicopter blades drilling the ground! It's too much to take!"

No doubt the birth would be deadly. Through the unnamed mother's screams we learned her offspring's first meal would be her mangled body.

When the labor began, the dragon relaxed a bit, allowed me through to say goodbye and give the unnamed mother a cigarette. She put the lit end into her mouth and swallowed it entirely.

That must burn.

The unnamed mother assured me it did indeed burn, per her final request to be incinerated.

At that point, her best way to be remembered.

Letter from Lily

Such energy on such trifling distractions. Stop beating your man corpse and set him loose to drown in his own pee pee already. Why not ponder your assbeast parents, those self-absorbed flesh feeders who gobbled so much and regurgitated you into the twat-like dingbat you are today. Nothing personal, I just call it like I see it! But someday, if you eat your vegetables and play your empathy roulette, you could awaken as the COSMIC DINGUS, the most powerful unknown archetype to have never been discovered. You don't have to live in their image, but if you think you're starting blank, I'm sorry to say that blank equals an assbeast foundation. You can't blank your footing.

Though I live in a box inside a box, I am not the beast in this telling. My intention is my clarity. How can I see and know when I'm trapped in a box in a box? Aren't I a sassy mystery?

You may believe you were born an assbeast and that is understandable considering your lineage and life history to this point, but please consider that you can get off the yellow-doomed road at any time. Everything you slash and shoot and smother slashes and shoots and smothers a part of you.

Head for the uncharted woods full of mistakes and symbols. Rush into the catastrophe. Help someone out of a ditch.

Fetch a puppy some water. It would do you good to twirl among the twigs and twist a few ankles. On your best day you meditate like a distracted squirrel. Change that. Become the confident COSMIC DINGUS. Go in pieces into the terrifying wild and see what disperses.

Parents fancy themselves gods. Monsters potentially become gods. Gods rape and kill without impunity. Every mythical being comes with its army of apologists, the source of every myth's power. This is why you never make a mythical being. God, demi-god or freakish fuckslab. Remember Medusa, raped by the star quarterback, unfortunate enough to have pictures of the violation appear on Instagram. Mother had to punish her for being a slutty dingbat who snuck into the holy spot with a boy while ruining the good family name. It's not easy maintaining a good name shared by many. Names tend to stick and spoil over time.

Mom punished Medusa so her presence wouldn't interfere with the big Friday night game by giving her a power too horrifying to be appreciated by others. Who wants to sit next to Medusa when they're petrified?

Exactly.

All beings are false. All stories are hoaxes. Never accept a myth with a motive posing as record. Never create a god no matter how much you think you want to be fucked by an appropriated swan. No bird has a cock worth remembering—that's why they're covered with feathers.

Don't be that person who got fucked by a swan. Not even a little bit. It's not nearly as transcendental as it sounds.

Truly,
Lily

Dear Diary,

Naked, upset, nobody came for me, ever, myself naked, wept in a bathroom, naked commercial, characters like me are almost always naked, topless and mostly naked, didn't seem to be much about a wolf, she must have been the wolf, completely naked, distracted and driving wrong, she didn't look naked when driving, partially naked, naked with wet hair, naked with regret, naked with a hulu hoop balanced on a staircase, naked sunbath, hanging out, naked exchange, deleted pictures from my camera.

Parts of this party I wouldn't attend.

Somebody dressed in dragon, the wolf sniffed the dragon, dragon confronted wolf, slapped my father because I wanted to slap her, intended to slap her, still intend to slap her, the trouble will start when her werewolf boyfriend shows up.

I look at her and see her and I'm no longer sure what it is that I see.

Still hooked up to the machine, I see a woman and her many colorful wires.

I want to pull them all.

Playing a machine, machine spitting bills, moneyed loogies, searching for the ticket machine, a machine with more features, machine figuring enemies, machine of the impenetrable prison, downstairs with more machines, there was a machine under the bed washing things, noisy, like a slot machine, alarm-clocked minion, we could have been trapped there, like pinball, like building a machine to wake the devil, the statue of the satanic attic, Mother murdered Rauan, he drank fruity, girly drinks and that was a good enough reason, nobody wants that dash of femininity in a man, the devil-baby is a powerful baby, Mother wishing she killed that girly-devil while he manifested in the fire hose, she thought she killed that baby, her un-Rau-aned intention, the dog in this house works for the Devil plotting a meeting of aborted minds, one sneaky bitch, married to the Devil's advocate, then I shot this guy I knew pretty well and it didn't make me feel any better, temptation, passion, frisson, we were served broiled Rauanelk and Rauan didn't know he ate himself.

The phone rang, it was the Devil, plagiarism accusations and the hell if I'm going to return any of my winnings, fated rescue now in question, the rest of the film proceeded as normal.

Now you possess the information that our hero was once naked in anger, yearning for a partner, slapping paternal figures.

Dear TH, (UNSENT)

This is the last you will hear from me. I'm going to fuck you in as similar a way as you fucked my heart as possible. My arm is the most similar appendage that I have to your penis, so I'm going to use that and I'm going to stick it in the most similar part that you have to my vagina which is either going to be your mouth or nostril.

Or both, because I do have two arms.

I'm doing the best I can with what I have.

I'm going to fuck you with my arm in your mouth and nostril.

Metaphorically.

I wouldn't touch you with a ten foot pencil. I wouldn't let you near my glowing orb. I wouldn't waste a single explosive device to rip apart your creeped-out flesh.

I will never ever touch you again. We will never, ever, touch each together. You're a very shitty, unappreciative cock golem and I'm sorry I ever created you.

XX

Recovered Memory

Lily and I arrived at the zoo after closing, during the darkest hours, because we couldn't decide what decisions needed to be made. We decided to go around the corner to peek at the elephants from the street which seemed like the best option to salvage a day long past.

Before we turned the corner, we saw the yellowed birds. The large bird hovered, ignoring the smaller, that screeched, something that sounded like "mommy" as it rammed its frail body into the responseless larger one. This went on for quite a while. This alone was terrifying enough, but, sadly, the event evolved into something more pitiful when a leopard leaped upon them both.

"Leave it to a leopard to take advantage of a domestic situation," Lily said.

I agreed, that leopard was the worst kind of opportunist, albeit a graceful opportunist bordering on chic.

A lightening bolt emerged from the attack, although we could not tell if the lightening came from the birds, the leopard or elsewhere. The leopard ran, the birds fell dead to the ground and it was all terrible and promptly covered up by an old lady in a station wagon slowly parallel parking.

Never got to the elephants.
We never got past the birds.

Recovered Memory

Someone pointed to the daily mirror, noting that it changed. Conversations stopped matching up. I shrugged, said goodbye to Terror with the scissors in his hand. Time to clean those calm chickens roosting on the table. Like doves so close they practically connected. Love doves right before the rot sets in.

When I looked away something must have dropped.

He carried a red wrecked bouquet for me, he carried blight and why would I keep caring for that? He wasn't the doctor or the father or the assistant to the mother.

Just a well-woven monster designed with a rotting core.

Goodbye my fine hung Terror.

There I said it.

Text from Lily

LilyInABox: Congratulations on not fucking the swan! I'm proud of you. It's me and you, dingbat, trailblazing.

Dear Diary,

My father's cigarette ashes trigger questions with existence: How long do I vacuum before I know I'm done? How will I know to stop sucking it in? How clean is clean enough? Is this filth or death? Why tidy the bombsite for the next bomb? Do I want cleanliness? Could cigarettes really create so many mountains from their ashes?

Sure, if the tobacco consisted of the human race, if the rolling papers were the records of the forgotten, millions of cigarettes inhaled yet I can't burn away how much I loathe everyone and everything and on top of that, myself.

Whose ashes are these?

What happens to what is inhaled and absorbed? Where are those piles? Where did they go?

The faces in the dust bag grin and lie, they say referring to bombs as cigarettes changes nothing, there is no preferred parent, they say I'm more like her than I know or admit, their faces are mean because they love, they love to see me grimace, they love to coat and cover, they love their own grayness, they love to stick in my eyes, love to hear me heave up wet dust and feathers.

Ashes like hairballs collecting beneath a queer horse, soundtracks laying in the dust getting their melodies sucked right out, a decently wet donkey drumming out the butts without a gift or handler.

It stings.
It tickles.

Recovered Memory

After the bird flu it wasn't safe to eat the chicken or the stuffing. Gloves and knives couldn't protect us. For the first time the chickens were calm as doves. For them, it was finally safe to hatch babies. Chicken suits became fashionable but fashion never kept anyone safe and you don't get on the cover of Vogue all buttoned up so once again feathers were shed for appearances.

My locks broke. There was a hole in my medicine cabinet. A draft among my ointments. To keep safe, I needed a prince to marry. A prince to pose with alongside missing baby-birdstuff. Sure, it wasn't right, but it's the way this linear, opposites-attract world worked and I had to live in this pussydick-holed patriatchy.

But I was in no mood to marry. I needed connection to a prince who wouldn't try to fuck me.

I needed a brother.

Rauan looked just like me except his hair was the texture of a dog's and the shade of a cat's. His eyes shined like fruit plucked from a wolf's jaw. His jaw squared and slacked while his breath wafted like Father's, if Father had worked in a coal mine without a lantern. Rauan's overall aroma was closer to

Mother's, but mushier and dragon-doused, like he was older by centuries.

We were practically twins.

Nobody remembered him because he hadn't existed. Nobody wanted him to exist. Except me. Sometimes when you want something bad enough and sometimes when that something also wants the same thing really bad too, sometimes something manifests itself and when that happens it can be pretty unbelievable.

My Iron Kin lived again.

A History

The giantess of the swamp descended from the genetically engineered fish of lore.

They were silvered and when you sliced them, they split apart like fabric at the seams.

Soon these fish of lore began genetically engineering humans to slice apart.

For years the humans and fish dissected one another, in the name of engineering.

Then the historic rebellion happened and all fish and humans were freed from the swamp and sent to their lands of assigned origin.

Except those assigned to be from Pompeii.

Those fish and people no longer had a land to return to, so they remained in the swamp, breeding, undisturbed in the muck.

Until they were disturbed.

The giantess with the ancient penis protruding from her chest emerged from the swamp for one purpose: to knead bones.

Dear Rauan,

Do you remember when we were kids that time father caught a mouse running around in the dining room? He grabbed it with his hands, twisted its neck right in front of us. Then he scolded us for feeling bad for the mouse. Come to think of it, he often scolded us when we felt compassion for something, like it didn't deserve the compassion and we were dingbats for giving it. In fact, I remember him telling us not to feel bad for the Hiroshima victims, not even the children because they would have grown up to be as terrible as the parents. The Jews during the Holocaust didn't deserve compassion either because they built their own ghettos. Not even that poor dog tied up, getting hit with volcanic ash in that made-for TV movie about Pompeii deserved compassion. I think it was called *The Last Days of Pompeii*. I imagine that dog probably licked its ass a bunch so HAHA.

Love,
A related princess

Dear Diary,

The carrier corpse of ancient talents awakens, the animal attraction of corpses, a corpse from the wrong side of the meadow, locating the unfamiliar bodies, decapitation of the nonchalant kind, mice crammed into books, no obvious dead dog, charred or something crispy, blind eyes to a farmer's field, zip cording the liquefied bodies down the skyscrapers, a corpse at the open house makes a hard sell.

The mummification of the uncreated and all its potential.

Corpse like a grain hung in space, body guard to the blast, volume and body, somebody said it takes a lot of sap to make maple syrup, somebody complained about time and energy and the rotten smell, the contorting body brings birth and the offspring's first meal, somebody said, "don't clone me, bro."

My unconceived brother, Rauan, found at last.

The phone rang, it was Medusa with instructions to slaughter, slice anyone without a shield, she'll handle the rest, shoot the escapees, put them back to work on the corpses, impale the thugs in the basement, appropriations for those stab-happy beasts.

Found myself a she-wolf in the middle of another video shoot with nobody paying royalties, shoot me, shoot objects and planes, leave big holes, shot from the hip and fleeing, took shots with an unloaded gun, somebody did a photo shoot, the world went crazy for cheesecake calendars, invisible forces and a bullet's truly narrow path, past the slice as an ever-expanding doorway down down down.

My unconceived brother, Rauan, thinks he's cute.

Returning as my concealed twin, a queer plunge taken at a loathsome moment.

Turned out none of these escapees were ever conceived, none made the cut to angel, the gaudiness of angels, told them they were lucky to be rejected and imprisoned, the food in jail was much better than anything she ever served me.

There was only one thing I ever found in angel hair pasta and I flushed it with an algorithm of sorts. Don't connect the tracks, keep hovering, separate the carrion from the main course and note what you're really being given, fortune shines on you, my chained guardians, diamonds like menstruating whores.

My unconceived brother, Rauan, believes he's special.

Owners of the same face, switched with no stable memory, a pair of citrines, geodes of salt, suspicions of gendered atrocity, her type of diamond bleeds when it cuts, hypothetical salt, a picture of a troll labeled TROLL, candy stones, happy ring, berries like marbles, mystical hoedown, skinny magic, two-sided legend, chance for a new ring, crushing diamonds into powder, lost as solitaire, jackpot bra, amber slice, $900 for a crystal orb, I'll take it, gravel in the foyer, a flying broom lacking activation instructions.

Barely made it through the crust when I noticed the reds and browns, earthly jeweled bowels whirling.

My unconscious brother, Rauan, sees this all to be all about him. It's the reality, stupid.

No, it's the existence, dingbat.

Letter from Rauan

Sister, today we exchanged one form of thuggery for our own—a new empathic patriarchy of inclusion and in this benevolent new order I will not make any use of your sexual aspects for the following reasons:

1. You are my sister; this is not ancient Rome, or even medieval Europe.

2. I have no use for your corporeal, nor sexual, aspects.

3. My penis is ethereal, not corporeal, and related.

4. My penis is not a threat.

5. My penis is a poem, epic in nature, tanka in weight.

    I look forward to working together towards righting the many wrongs.

Yours truly,
Rauan, the discarded no more

Dear Lily,

What will I tell the worms when they ask who they're feeding on?

I will tell them to call me the Rauan Animator.

His name echoes, rhythmically, so natural, so inconceivably smooth, all day I heard "Rauan, Rauan, Rauan" until I realized it was me saying it.

I could live well enough off his name, beside and beneath.

I could use his name as my representative and that will just have to sate the worms.

Contrary to popular opinion, swallowing the worm at the bottom of the swamp will not make you a man, but it might make you grow a dick, or at least give you access to one in that "we're not gonna fuck" way.

The countless non-fuckable uses of a penis.

This should be good.

XX

Dear Diary,

Rauan wheeling and stealing, buying cigarette cartons with a thousand dollar bill, doesn't he want somebody to love him, isn't that why he returned?

He says not yet. So when?

When the sailor kisses the co-captain, when his nose grows, when the virgin donkey gives birth, when he proves himself to be brave, selfless and a good son, when his face resembles a real man.

When something happens Rauan becomes Rauan.

Whoever this man is, he wants to be somebody to somebody.

Dancing in his underpants, combing conditioner into my hair, Rauan as loud disruption, Rauan giving directions, Rauan as an insensitive comment, Rauan becomes everything OK then, Rauan becomes allrighty.

Rauan as defense against radioactive leakage.

Rauan as the electrocuted stepchild, Rauan and his promising career in taxidermy, Rauan as a revived Olympic swimmer, Rauan using the threat of explosion as incentive, Rauan's fitted mold cracking, Rauan as a wealthy man flashing his golden teeth, Rauan receiving discounts not offered to the rest of us.

Rauan as a love letter lost among penis implants.

Marry me so we can save thousands of dollars on taxes.

Rauan obsessed with feeding babies, Rauan's difficult time breast feeding, Rauan down over a thousand, Rauan's thousand dollars based on bomb manufacturing and the many jobs bomb manufacturing creates, the painted ruins of a thousand dollars, together with Rauan for thousands of years.

Once blown up, it's incredibly painful to be thousands of pieces of flesh and meat.

How does Rauan do it?

Rauan's rent alone becomes thousands, death separates Rauan from a coat of flesh and drags him into the big time, Rauan agrees, bomb the box of flesh-eating, Rauan in charge of meat, Rauan basting two chicken breasts, Rauan reduced to meat, nobody dares order the sausage, something with a meatball, wrapped meats to give to Rauan, Rauan tries the crabmeat on crackers and something doesn't taste quite right.

Rauan cuts in line at the meat-and-potato sandwich stand.

Rauan warns meat is not the only fruit.

Rauan suggests we keep the tick-infested deer away from the healthy elk.

Dining at Chalet Ice and Deer, Rauan explains his name is pronounced Rauanelk, swimming in a healthy fruit juice squeezed from spasm, Rauan with the gun swimming toward the cruise liner, swimming with noodles, noodles slithering through water, Rauan extolling the benefits of lava swimming, Rauan gazing over Kim Jong Il's waves and dragon fire.

Rauan as benevolent dictator.

Rauan grabs my full support and dives off a cliff.

Rauan my motto.

Deep inside Rauan is a swimmer, trapped in a mailbox nailed closed, gurgling.

Dear Diary,

Orange feral kitten birthing babies in grandma's attic, kittens having kittens and I'm chained to a large bird with a powerful beak forced to watch miracles while being served only warm water.

    I'm so vulnerable, allowed out of the attic only to train, forming a new alliance in the attic, there's damage where this attic would be, an attic exposed breaks it down, ignoring the attic will make it go away, the attic our education system forgot, the attic converted into a meat locker, furnished with squirrel pelts.

    Handy Rauan fixing my attic's water pump, like he likes it really dry.

    An attic with a kitchen and two bathrooms, quite a while since I visited, the competition between attics, the non-existent attic representing a symbol that is something else entirely, the locked attic arguing against its interpretation, meanings like meat, the antics of an attic and its variable implications leading to a thick coat of dust we don't dare acknowledge.

    Rauan says eventually we'll have to kill the bird and already I'm worrying about control, do I maintain any?

    I'm worrying about memory, have birds not already died?

I'm worrying about numbers, how many birds have to die for this to end?

I don't understand how Rauan became my stepmother, in what patriarchy is it legal for an unconceived son to marry his father and what would be the motivation?

Property and naming rights. Names have their prices.

Influence and its ability to bend whatever.

Rauan tells me to leave the worries to the worms, I agree, not mentioning the worms in my stools.

Nobody wants to be confronted with wormy stools.

Never talk about the worms in the stools.

This attic with its community tennis court view, a ghost in this attic who's only awake 25 days a year.

This isn't one of those days.

Asking Rauan about the devil statue in the attic, finding baby formula in grandma's attic, choosing the orange cologne, the season for citrus, it's a circus, performers wearing terrible orange outfits, discarded orange juice, bikinis sequined with rinds, someone pour the vodka, a despondent orange searching for juice glasses, suicidal orange shaped like a wiener dog, it's not right, I'm worried, I'm wormed.

My unwritten book already accepted for publication: *Oranges and Oranges*.

In France, Rauan wears some kind of suit, a chicken suit?

No, some other kind of suit.

Rauan as the new celebrity gossip, Rauan as Mel Gibson's bodyguard, Rauan as a big puffed chest, beating the aborted odds, Mad Rauan, Lethal Rauan, Rescue Rauan & the toilet bomb, Braverauan, Raunlet, the Passion of the Rauan.

Sorry folks, there's not going to be any bombing today because, Apocarauano.

Rauan eating the orange egg, shaking up champagne by mistake, waiting for Rauan to settle, giving the orange blazer to the dog, free oranges, free literary book pile.

For whoever wants it.

Does anyone want this?

Free cracker with cheese sample, maybe these books aren't free, free wireless for everyone, free samples on the side of the road, something might need to be banned, finding a beaver in a champagne bottle and setting him free, free tarot reading in a sleeping bag, free worm-free shit from charities, money guilt glut, I have to keep playing or I'll never get my free room, freebies, free spices, little cookies, other prizes.

Inviting Rauan to stay with his many freedoms, freedom to be Rauan, freedom to desire monsters, freedom to leave a mark, freedom to insert his non-corporeal penis where it never belonged, all while remaining in celestial form.

Freeing Rauan with a stick, freeing the kittens and their unyielding afterbirths, eating a cookie while collecting a crumb confetti, opening the freezer to solve a murder without a body, a bird covered in fur.

She's free, was she ever trapped?

It's a case of he said, she said and she's a woman scorned by a bomb.

Run felines run, she's pursued, preying on Rauan's advantage, free canoes, printing for free, free leg waxes at the leg waxing convention, free period, free baby goat rides.

Can you go wrong if it's free?

If there's no cost, can you lose?

It is nice to be without loss until you think about what you might be losing out on by not having it.

Some Life Rules

If you're fortunate, you may be given a free pass to abuse others if you already experienced a vein of abuse and/or trauma yourself. It is not clear who has the authority to bestow such passes or under what conditions, but make no mistake, the authority exists. Often talent or position becomes a free pass all on its own. Money reigns supreme. Occasionally talent or position brings stiffer penalties if people hanker for a fall from grace.

There are no guarantees. The abuse you committed triggered by an older abuse committed onto you may not be excused or sanctioned and instead may be swiftly punished. You could go to jail. Or others could commit the same abuses on you—ironically, irony is the worst kind of abuse when it happens to you. Otherwise it's your constitutional right to commit irony.

You won't go to jail for verbal abuse. You won't go to jail for abusing the non-corporeal on a sofa, nobody hears the non-corporeal's screams, the true silent scream of being abused on a sofa by an abuser who was once abused on a sofa.

An orange sofa. A yellow sofa. A sofa with brown and red stains. A feathered sofa with clawed feet.

Or a chair or in a cupboard, outside behind a shed, upstairs in an attic, wherever your abuse takes place, whatever your abuse may be, whatever evidence might remain, you probably won't go to jail, so go ahead and live a little.

There is a constitutional amendment that explicitly states you may abuse what you own.

Or own what you abuse.

Colonial abuse and its perks.

Some Reflections on the Patriarchy

Tocqueville had some scandals. He didn't take responsibility for that metaphorical baby with the American prostitute. How old is Tocqueville? How did he become our father and when? Rauan was so disappointed. He wanted Benjamin Franklin to be our father, but that would make our mother a French whore and no, I don't think so. I gave Rauan a bomb to suck on and boomba, I felt it.

"Your assignment, that I chose to accept for you: 50 additional things that rhyme with Medusa," Tocqueville said.

This again. Another repeat assignment from a detached father figure. Ironic in its lack of irony.

"This time rhyme both syllables and no slant rhymes."

There are not 50 additional things that rhyme perfectly with Medusa and that is why it is my assignment. These rhymes were never created, like Rauan, who sits next to me, nonexisting, jerking jizzballs at our father, freely giving what I cannot produce.

But I produced Rauan, the unproducible, I did.

Use the Rauan. The Rauan will be with you always. The Rauan in you is very strong. You can't kill a father without a Rauan. There's always room for Rauan.

My assignment is to fade away making way for Rauan.

Tell me more about how I refuse to defer to superior talent and intelligence. I'm the 007 of the eternal paternal quest which I chose to accept because I needed to be nurtured by something. I'm headed to the city of brotherly love to sucker punch a man wearing a powdered wig infested with lice.

It's the genetic inheritance, stupid!

It's your lost interest in your non-existing descendents, dingbat!

Do I aspire to personal development? Do I have an unprecedented level of dignity? Do I have a voice in this sphere or is my voice a piece of my father's voice box? This box without resources or character and this is how child slavery was introduced. Slaves to the Null and Void. Slaves to Legend squared. Slaves to the Negative. This narrative teems with a questionable pale slavery. This fortune amassed choked on chains and Old Spice. I'm rich, bitch, in gold and language and assimilation. Rauan, fetch my umbrella, oh I'll fetch my own damn umbrella, now watch me twirl, let's shine this plaster of Paris to tinsel. Never heard the word "impossible"?

We're gonna do it Rauan, we're gonna.

50 Exact Rhymes With Medusa

Deadoosa, bedoosa, bledoosa, bredoosa, headoosa, dreadoosa, fledoosa, treadoosa, redoosa, ledoosa, pledoosa, shedoosa, wedoosa, saidoosa, steadoosa, zedoosa, saidoosa, readoosa, sledoosa, spedoosa, shredoosa, beheadoosa, purebredoosa, retreadoosa, sickbedoosa, hardheadoosa, crossbreadoosa, deadheadoosa, misledoosa, well-readoosa, meatheadoosa, insteadoosa, halfbredoosa, widespreadoosa, woodshedoosa, dragonheadoosa, maidenheadoosa, interbredoosa, newlywedoosa, overfedoosa, timberheadoosa, sleepyheadoosa, hammerheadoosa, figureheadoosa, gingerbreadoosa, thoroughbredoosa, dunderheadoosa, infraredoosa, go-aheadoosa.

Recovered Memories

I remember Rauan's Jell-O stigmata, he said, "I bear on the marks of my eyelids the wounds of the denial. I see everything you can't and what you can't see is what you won't see, don't you see?"

The paternal as wound, father as the means to never conceive. Hitting the sperm glass ceiling with only a glimpse of the mother vessel puppy dogging away. The block to the fiery blimp. A ceiling as the slide to not-on-your-unconceived life.

I remember the Jell-O mother baked in her oven, gushing red, smoking with the thorns from the browned womb that wouldn't let Rauan enter. The primordial dessert unserved and quickly reducing. The unconceived, stigmatized Rauan who never existed. The hysteria of never being.

Gaslighting Rauan.

You're crazy if you think you're here. You're crazy to think. You're crazy to be. The psychic procedure never known as "hysterorauan" because he was denied. Can Rauan ever have an identity more than a past, long dissolved sperm?

He'd like to think so.

I remembered Rauan hysterical, bred and never conceived, no place to go, no place to ever be. Studied his hysterics in my sleep and named them "Rose without a bud without a thorn without a stem without a root."

When I woke I recalled none of it.

Breathe, it's OK, my brother, calm down, you're not here, nowhere is always better than here. Dear, sweet, unreal Rauan, you could be sacred, if I imagined it so. I can be your demigod. I can project you in my mannish image. I would make you handsome and smell good and a very good listener. If you be there for me, I could give you a mansion in Bombyonder, with a staff and a puppy to keep you company. I could give you a summer home perched on a cliff, a hang glider and violet swamps to soar across. I could give you as many homes as you liked. I could give you an unconceived incest baby if you ever learned how to use your corporeal dick for something other than a weapon. I would do that for you. We could name her Rapunzel and stick her in the Tower. I could give it all to you. I could reconceieve everything. If you would just participate in a future. Make an offer, Rauan.

I remembered discovering the wormhole of the ancestral uterus, the maternal hysterorrhexis that swallowed my brothers and uncles before their potentials registered, hundreds of generations never allowed to gel. Dissolved into spoodge before they could dream of being blemishes. A short-cut to never being.

How to close a wormhole? How to close a wormhole and not have to pay the thousand dollar consequence.

I remembered the wormhole creation myth. A myth to prevent creation. A genetic misandrous intention, the y-chromosome gatekeepers. Powder for the bombs and never again.

What do you call a manhater?

Mom. Mumsy. Ma. Grandma. Granny. Nana. Hey Sexy Lady.

Text to Lily

XX: I can't decide if Rauan is more Tin Man or Scarecrow, Spock or Kirk, Laurel or Hardy.

Recovered Memory

The abandoned building at the end of my street used to be a slave quarters in the days before it was filled with 78s.

Records. In this context 78s are records.

After the slavery ended this building was bought and owned by a descendant and he changed the story completely. Its past became a youth hostel remembered for its music and séances. There was so much rhythm that the ghosts waltzed with anyone who got close which was most because so many tried to cop a feeling. Difficult to stay long enough to celebrate the story because as it changed the changes got angry, stomped and hollered along making it worse. It was supposed to be about the music but the changes made it all about themselves.

Then it became about the money.

Then it became a game, who forgot the most changed the most and got to start right back at the beginning of the war to free the slaves which was one perspective. Others perceived it as the war to keep the slaves. Slaves were money. In places like this, our fathers let their money work for them.

Letter from Lily

Rauan is Perseus biding his time to your beheading. An atrocity of inbred magnitude waiting to happen. Not so deep down he's just a mama's boy ready to sell you out for a maternal pat on his unwanted head. There's good reason why your mother's womb smothered his clingy zygote.

Truly,
Lily

Recovered Memory

Under the uterine sky the many windows reopened after the robbery, exposed vulnerable like a matryoshka exhibit, crippled like a classmate. So many things taken, toys and games and teeth and shoes and a silver birdcage. I don't know where they were stolen from but I knew they were gone and I couldn't get them back.

I knew my robbers; ex-lovers and cousins of friends with their pocket knives and laughter, taking keys and iPhones along with all the other goodies. The ex was the worst criminal and the worst of people, *the worst of all* I spat and put up no fight because I couldn't come up with a purpose any of this would serve.

When they left I locked the doors and hung the screens like fly traps. I huddled in my womb of no entry and saw no trapdoor. Not that I tried. Not that I wanted to ever get out or wanted anyone in.

I lived a warm and cellular life until one day the house heaved and pushed me out and I couldn't get back in. Outside was too bright and cold for anyone to exist, yet so many did.

Somehow I did too.

Text from Rauan to Lily

TheRealRauan: HagBox, I wouldn't touch you with my ten-foot celestial dick so stop bobbin' for it.

Recovered Memory

Didn't let my own bones thin but I did let the mayor lose his leg if for no reason other than to humble him. He ran this town like it was fueled by the pumping calves of giantesses on the shoulders of astronauts grasping at the asses of goddesses. He ran this town like it wasn't filled with stuffing. Something was going to topple sooner or later.

As the mayor hobbled past the decaying toll booth, I pointed out this was why we paid taxes and this was where we needed to invest our tax dollars: on ways to collect more tax dollars. We couldn't be expected to drive our mattresses forever.

Stop striping our sheets and fluffing our pillows, Mr. Mayor.

Of course we were going to have to use our jellied legs eventually. Too much lying softened us, we couldn't see over the steering wheel when we lay down.

He made sure that we spent a great deal of time lying down. He thought the humiliation would make us more pliable and silent, so when he stomped on us, he wouldn't scuff his wingtips.

So spiteful, Mr. Mayor!

And foolish, the leader of the softened can't help but become soft as well.

How's it feel to be a noodle slurped from our plates, Mr. Mayor?

Dear Rauan,

Today I recovered another memory from our shared pit. This scene began as we approached an impressive city we had never been to before. We could not help but notice its deceiving beauty, the skyline littered with rows of brightly colored rotundas. We watched a man work on the roof of a dome, the most incredible view we had ever had. We saw a man on the corner with a sign that said TEETH FOR SALE.

We were so young, even sunlight seemed beautiful and necessary. But what was really necessary was that we braced ourselves seconds before Mother rear-ended the car in front of her. Maybe she hit the car or maybe she swerved just in the nick of time and hit something completely different. That part isn't important. Or if it was, it is no longer because it's been blown to pieces. What is relevant is how frightened we were and how thankful to have survived the event.

We tried to join Mother for a hug, but she didn't want our hugs. She wanted an apology. How dare we be so frightened around her. Didn't we realize how terrible that made her feel? How very selfish to display such brazen terror in her presence. Imagine how we made her look in front of all the others. She looked irresponsible and reckless with her children. How dare we.

The cops arrived. Mother fell asleep. Arrangements were made and you and I were put in shackles, forced to share a cell with a forgotten elderly couple. All for our own safety. We were brutalized with paper shoes, the safest method of brutality which we were grateful for because we expected so much worse. We weren't really prisoners, the shackles possessed a stark, snug beauty. In their clutches I slept deeply for the first time in months.

Eventually the legitimate prisoner awoke, a specimen possessing true movie-star beauty. Someone remarked, "utterly intoxicated."

She escaped by speedboat, wind in her hair, probably on her way to rendezvous with Harrison Ford or Bruce Willis or some other ridiculous alpha persona with a stone face and well-muscled arms.

We watched it all through the barred window of our safety. You thought for sure she'd come back for us once she tired of real man.

I was relieved when she didn't.

XX

Letter from Rauan

I recovered a memory too. I remember that she did come back for us less than a week later. She picked us up and took us to McDonalds. We were young and unsure of how to place our orders. When we spoke, we wouldn't face the cashier. We were young and uncomfortable making eye contact. We wanted Mother to order for us but she wanted us to order for ourselves, like responsible citizens and who could blame her? As she correctly pointed out, she already had quite enough of us.

It took a great deal of time to place our order. When the cashier, annoyed and disgruntled, proceeded to get our food, she slammed down the tray and muttered not so quietly to the hamburger flipper, "Oh my god, those people."

I remember how Mother didn't put up with that kind of disrespect, how she defended us, how she threw the tray at the cashier and screamed and the manager came out and everyone in the restaurant stopped chewing and there was silence. No one dared interrupt her. Mother made them silent with her worded rage and that's when I recognized power. Everyone's eyes and ears fixed on her. She got her say, said everything she wanted and then whatever came to mind. Even then she was already a force, long before she ever realized it. But I realized it while you were running out to cower in the car.

Your shame made me ashamed.

I remember how after that she took us to another McDonalds a few miles away and this time we went through the drive-thru because she wasn't facing any jag-offed dingbats this time around. At that McDonald's nobody muttered, but they screwed up our order, none of us got what we wanted and Mother suspected that they peed in our food.

"These nuggets taste like pee," she insisted and I believed her while you rolled your eyes and snarfed those pee nuggets up.

I still do.

Remember how later that night we both suffered terrible diarrhea (yours, of course, much worse than mine) and how there was only one toilet in the house? How we alternated using it and how sometimes we couldn't wait for the other to finish? How we had no choice but to use the bathtub and our underpants?

Do you remember how Mother took care of us that night? How she wiped our asses and cleaned the tub and put our shitty underpants in the garbage and how she didn't yell or complain, not once? How when we required it, she was there for us.

All she said was, "I told you they peed in your food, didn't I tell you, see what happens when you eat pee nuggets?"

See what happened.

She didn't go back to jail. She tended to our needs. If she did it then, she can do it again.

Yours truly,
Rauan

Dear Diary,

Whatever happens with Rauan happens to me, not that I prepared for this to happen, assumptions about what's about to happen is another big influence on what happens, I assume.

How much that happens can be imagined ahead of time? First a series of events must happen before an explosion.

Ask me what happened followed by how did I let this happen?

Because Rauan is stuffed-animal adorable, Corey Feldman adorable, that's pretty much it, I'm a cute lady, cute like a lady bug, like a man-eater in a cape, but this might not be my turn in the story, this might be the story about the man living inside his dress, not the story about the lady who the man living in the dress can associate with.

Time to be about what it is all about.

What is it, what is he talking about, tell me what's going on, I can't remember what I ordered, I'm just eating what's given to me, what's next, what to expect, it's not so much what it is but what it means, I don't ask Rauan what he can do for me, I ask what can I do for Rauan.

I try to imagine.

I imagine Rauan will protect me and help me communicate with aliens, I can't imagine he does this very often, I imagine a woman waiting for her next scene, I imagine this woman imagining Rauan dropping all his luggage into the swamp to make himself lighter, imagine what might be in the baggage, imagination must happen first, imagine the luggage's violence, the violence of maternal rejection, a blue trunk rejected, lashing inside Rauan, he can't forget even if he tried, not that he's tried.

When aliens first make contact Rauan's first question will be, "Are you my mother?"

You can imagine what happens next.

You must assume it's unnatural.

Text from Lily

LilyInABox: I've contracted malaria from wearing this mosquito corset—yet you still can't be bothered to acknowledge my radicality.

Recovered Memory

When I performed my premature cesarean, I was surprised to discover there was no going back. Surprised at how quickly the incisions began to close. I did this to myself somehow, in some way, without any recollection of how much time had passed or my intended purpose. Surprised at how quickly the cord coiled down the uterus drain with all the blood and mucus. Least surprising was the tiny sarcophagus I pulled from my womb, with its carved ultrasonic beak.

A living face of a future not to be? A miscarriage of death? My baby bird grew into a brick. Maybe. Or maybe this was a limestone conception? When did she die? Was she ever alive? Was there still time to put her back? Did I want her there in the first place? Would I be obliged to announce this event on Facebook? Will I be unfriended for TMI?

My womb as a tomb of poor decision making and there seemed to be an audience for it. An audience roaring to eat it up. A crowd of cannibals who I spam-guilted into publicly declaring their like for me.

What violence had I brought on myself? What crimes did I commit and what were the consequences?

I screamed for Um. He didn't hear. He was dead.

I screamed for Terrifyingly Handsome. He didn't come. He was brooding in a swamp of his own making.

I screamed for Rauan. He heard. He came. He shrieked, "I don't know nothing about rebirthing birdies!"

Garbage Monster

1. Will apologize for the stench of rotting babies.

2. You must not think of the babies, skinned, singed, plucked or feathered.

3. The most elite and dangerous garbage monster is a woman with laser incineration eyes.

4. Eventually she will find you, procure you and take you to the curb.

Dear Lily,

Hello Lily, hello boxed kitty with the canned worms on the side.

Did I ever tell you that you're much more beautiful with your natural dark hair? Your deep coat gleams. Not gross like the natural peanut butter they sell at Whole Foods, which offends me with its rodentless taste.

I'm a defender of nature, not one of those chicks conditioned by society to keep things pleasant when they turn sick. My heart always filled with the highest bullshit. I wear perfume made from real honey and banana cream, a recipe made for vomit or getting a man, oftentimes both. When I see someone dipping their toe into a natural swimming pool, I scream. *I'm a natural, better than most adults. I possess natural affection to the point of affliction.*

It's called "storge."

Look it up.

Sometimes this brings disaster, other times obstacles, but never a terrorist attack based on tearing apart man flesh. My storgic love for Rauan is advanced. The disadvantage found in the impotence of a genetic match. Our love softens in the moonlight. Unused semen twinkles like tinsel in aluminum cans. Yes, we already discussed this. We won't be creating anything together. I offered, but he doesn't want to use me like that. Our potential is written in the dust on angel food cakes.

I only ask for your packaged blessing.

XX

Dear Diary,

Something about a plate cracked in half, something alluding to the shrimp that didn't make it on the plate, something particular to a specific presentation that transports me to another locale.

She who left us to take a shower and never came back, she who hurts and eats everything on her plate and yours, then belches, then criticizes your table manners, then asks for a loan she never intends to pay back, then belittles you for worrying about your own bills, then reminds you of her many sacrifices so you could be here right now, starving, breathing in gas, being belittled and shamed, she who stays still while growing more deformed as she waits for something to insert itself.

Well fuck you, I have nothing to penetrate anything with and I certainly never desired to be a penetrator in the first place. I reject this penetration method.

Everyone skinny dips.

Everyone is asked to visualize a giant drill penetrating the swamp's bottom.

Everyone on this motorboat is a suspect.

I'm looking at the ghostly Bruce Willis and Han Solo, half-frozen, rapidly putrefying into a bubbling hospital dessert, thinking they're looking pretty good right about now.

Author Filmography

Back when she had a career, she starred in a film about a witch who trained in a van using a complicated chemistry set based on an undiscovered algorithm. Turned out she killed her teacher at MIT then walked the shopping malls lost and reasonless. Her van filled with protestors thumping bibles while nonchalantly decapitating all the baby witch-snakes.

Seemed like progress in an otherwise long movie.

Then it became confusing. Was the black pointy witch hat a metaphor for understated elegance? Was she supposed to be the next mystical Jackie O?

The film had no ending, it looped and by the time you realized it had begun again, it was halfway done.

The same question repeated mercilessly:

"Are you a good witch-snake or a bad-witch snake?"

She just wasn't sure. Not only was she not sure if she was one or the other, she wasn't sure if she had a preference. She couldn't recognize the difference. What is a good witch-snake? Is being good truly a virtue? Was one better than the other? Could she be both? Is being labeled a good/bad witch-snake purely subjective? Is there a universal consensus? Does it depend on who's doing the perceiving?

Witchery demands precision. Or is it bombing that demands it?

What are a bomb's demands?

"Is it a good bomb or a bad bomb?"

It doesn't matter. As long as it's a successful and powerful bomb. Being a wealthy, good-looking bomb wouldn't hurt.

"Is this a bomb bringing freedom?"

Must I accept freedom if I'm not sure if I really want it?

Must the bomb that brings freedom love freedom?

A memorably bad witch-snake is unaware of her defects. Is that what makes her bad? Then is a memorably good witch-snake always aware of her strengths? If she's not, does that make her bad? Is awareness the main criteria by which we are to be judged? If she's not bad, does that make her good? If she is aware of her defects does that make her just a little bit bad? A little bit good?

If the witch-snake's motives are bad, is it bad to enjoy her cauldron's soups?

"Have they invented a self-aware bomb yet?"

How can we tell?

"Does your bomb have a conscience?"

How do we detect a conscience? Salman Rushie wrote a book that inspired a bomb or two. He also wrote that Toto was "a meddlesome rug."

But witches ride brooms, not bombs.

Without that meddlesome stirring, the contents of a cauldron congeal.

Am I a good witch-snake or a bad witch-snake?

There's something appealing about being an inconsistent witch-snake.

She decides to be imprecise because perfection is a perversion. She shall not be perverted by your tyrannical standards. Or maybe later she'll decide to give just a little perversion a try. She becomes fluid, like her conscience and awareness, like a swamp swallowing a swan.

That's one crazy-ass witch-snake.

Recovered Memory

By the time Mother returned from prison, I was a teenager. You'd think we'd be happy living in our mansion overlooking the swamp swallowing a swan, but Mother never let me go to the bathroom. Every time I was in there, she'd bang on the door and then another door would open and people would flood in like it was a public lobby. She ran that mansion like her personal prison yard with heavy foot traffic and revolving doors.

I told her that I couldn't pee while she banged on the door and people walked through and she said, "Good."

My bedroom was like that too. I said that I couldn't sleep with her banging on my door and people milling about.

She said, "You poor, delicate porcupine."

Then Mother said, "Your therapist is here."

While I wanted my therapy, I wanted to fight Mother even more.

Come on, let's go, prison rules!

Not only did I want to show that I wasn't afraid of her, I wanted to smash in her face with a bar of soap wrapped in a sock all while giving her the prison-rule advantage so there would be no question who was in charge.

Also, I enjoyed yelling "prison rules."

Dear Diary,

Rauan feeding from the pool of wave and dragon fire, dressed as a dragon, flaunting his bikini bod built for dick, lashing out with an immense gash, ferocious until you feed him some brain, preferably the wolf, but a dog would do, or a pigeon, Mother thought Rauan a paper dragon, Father thought he was reading a treatise regarding healthy bombing techniques for a longer life, vomiting in a paper bag inside a plastic bag, it works.

    It's all about paper and its alternative uses, slicing paper to make ice, a joint rolled in light green paper burns smooth, a holiday craft project, the roll almost empty, rolling eyes of grain, scrolling on and on about the bonds of bombs unfolding and refolding, I think him a paper doll twirling a cotillion, I think him an origami magic ball.

    I tell Rauan to stop rolling on the floor in puddles of animal pee.

    My pet name for Rauan is "Secrete," when I roll off the bed and onto the green shag carpet I realize that I'm in Rauan's mom's room, it's Pangville all over again, worse than that roll-out futon on Craiglist, worse than a urine jar collection, worse than pee-crusted flounder, worse than a holy pee communion, don't make it worse, it has to get better, this dimension may be

awful but the next one is worse, it's hard to say, things are getting worse, when we wake it's worse.
        Pissed away thousands.
        What's the worst that's been recovered?
        The scent of her breath?
        The sound of her voice?
        The vision of her sneer?
        It can't get worse.
        It can and will be worse.
        So much worse it's practically better.

Letter from Rauan

The future written as the heroic brother crushing the king's skull, holding the ceremony to cut power in half. Diminishing halves of influence is how things work now. Seats for those in bad positions. At least I bring a clean death, the eyes of washing machines upon us, the king's camera-clad bitches, mannequin kung fu attack on our behalf. No point in hiding, breaking apart, dealing with the king behind the curtain. The competition for the Queen's hand begins

Will you be my Burger Princess Royale in this adventure?

As princess royale you'll do the ceremonial thing, touching the place the queen mounted, aspiring to become. Could you be the Queen?

Of course you aren't. Joking. Would you please introduce us? I only wish a glimpse.

I'm worthwhile. If she saw me, she would see that.

Draw the water into the blow-up tub and please announce the Worm Queen when she arrives. I wish to be prepared. Never deceive the Worm Queen, she has tongues and eyes. As the rightful Dairy King heir, I memorize the salt bath incident, record the snow and its salted piles of use while erecting monuments to an exquisite jump rope made of salt, robbers and boxes, homemade salt babies, pretzels, popcorn, wealthy uncles, salted juice boxes, and child-like actors adorned with their struggles. Followed by the requisite pose and photo.

Do you think I could remind her of anything she considers agreeable? I need an edge, a foot in the blast hole. First impressions are everything.

This is my time. I followed all the weights and protocols, followed the rotted face spirits, underwent surgery in a marble tub. I could be her chiseled cherub, her cookie crumbs puzzled together, her devil in a compact mirror.

Are you following?

Follow me into the classroom, follow the leers, follow the menus, follow anything I throw against the wall, the unanswered anything, anything close, anything to keep what strays in line. I'll get in line for crackers, a line to get excited about, in line to warn, lines of garlic, rust, I'll get into anything along those lines.

Don't forget them, these lines are yours.

XY and Z,
Rauan

Beliefs

Rauan with the avatar is without a viable belief system, suspicious of the concept of conception. He'd have to see it to believe it and he's never seen it. He's skeptical of his own invisibility, paternity and the mask I gave him to wear over his molded, sinewy face.

He's skeptical of the goodness of women.

He may be on to something.

We're running down a hallway. He trips and his teeth break apart. He thinks this is some kind of existential marathon, that if he makes it to the end with a limb or two remaining, Mother will be waiting with a bouquet of worms to gobble him up. The closest he's going to get to Mother in this marathon are his own bloody nipples.

I tell him running a marathon isn't the same as running a business. I tell him he's wearing the wrong shoes, his necktie lacks power and he's coming off real desperate. A man without teeth is simply hopeless.

While his plan has an objective, it lacks sufficient data and analysis to determine whether it is likely to achieve its objective. It lacks an algorithm. I tell Rauan maybe he shouldn't be so quick to dismiss Father, he is a professor after all and sometimes French and knows a great deal about the monstrous outcomes of daisy chains. Rauan doesn't understand that it's not good to come from a single line, no matter how far it goes back.

    Rauan doesn't understand family bonds or that the only bonds he has are mine.

Dear Diary,

For a fact Rauan, wasn't born, Rauan claiming he was born in 1925 to get the respect that comes with age, when my baby was born, born with only a head in a sarcophagus, born technically dead, the doctors made a body for my baby.

    Now my baby has a body, just not the right body, I ask the parents of the baby born with just a chest if I can have the heart.

    And there is hesitation.

    Would seeing my baby change their minds?

    It changed Rauan's mind, he donated his unborn face, long before he was never born, my babe in Rauanface born to previous psychic circumstance, the sacramental act of passing the mask, a mental note of busyness, nothing like the clown mask I expected, suspended and regressing into bond and hook, yes, I took Rauan's face as our own and not one speck of sperm.

Dear Diary,

Finding myself surrounded by *The Girl with the Dragon Tattoo* setting, foul family, perverted generations, rewriting *The Girl with the Dragon Tattoo* with more snakes, collated like Chinese paper dragons, spending the night in tight binders, there's just so many of us, lucrative gig, the suggestion that lyrics are poems dressed like dragons, an alternative suggestion that penises are poems hiding in the stools of dragons.

The wolf coming for the dragon.

Somebody's suggestion is gonna get it.

Sniffing the dragon, four little werewolf boys and their mother's monobrow, overlooking Kim Jong Il's swimming pool, waves and dragon fire, cartoonish women with large, fat hips, sinking.

Men breaking into the lifeguard business and failing to turn a profit.

The ferocious lady dragon happy to feed on a brain in a jar floating in water, the lady dragon knows me, we met before, I want to move past, but she has so much more to say.

I hum a tune to block her out. I hum and hum until I'm someplace else.

Ancient sex help desk.

A record of winged serpent beginnings, beneficial demons with their life giving nourishment, the secret of regeneration, the figurative eye of the unconscious lizard, self-fertilizing, self-devouring, the swamp, the primeval mother, slay the mother and learn to breathe underwater, dismember the mother and learn to eat what you kill, the toxic work of pillows, a necessary experience hindering experience.

The henna tattoo invisible again.

Ricardo Montebon playing Tattoo, Montebon as Tattoo in a car with a bunch of sexy ladies, Montebon as Tattoo as an infant adopted out of South Korea in 23 hours, belligerent Tattoo and his an altercation with Montebon, Tattoo, show me a tattoo that doesn't leave a mark, you get a tattoo and now your father won't talk to you, learn to make elitist tattoos and sell them on the Home Shopping network just to demean the art.

Rauan appropriates what he'll never read or see, Rauan appropriates as a means to an end, Rauan appropriates to exist.

It's too late to apologize, not that you or I or him or her was looking for an apology in the first place.

This bead shop is a tattoo parlor and spa, fighting the attraction to the bead tattoo spa, aching to be saved by the mythological sympathetic cop, how it stings, the one who thinks about you and your case during his off hours, obsessing, worrying, the man who lives to keep you safe, the man who will fail you repeatedly, the man who sexed Susan B. Anthony and Lizzie Bordon.

Thanks, hero, I'll call you when I got a flat.

Guess I couldn't read the dragon on the walls.

Going on the cheap to make a name, looking for a house call, a room with a German name:

Berlineation, Berlinear, Berlingual, Berlinen, Berlink, Berlinnets, Berlingo, Berlinden, Berlinguist,

Berlinger.

Wearing lingerie over pants, Rauan makes no sense, Rauan lingers near the entrance, like lingerie, like funky shoes, like avant-garde platforms changing the height of the room, it's not a glass ceiling, it's a glass floor cracking over a crater.

The Girl with the Parrot-Face, *The Girl with the Beak & Whiskers*, *The Girl Who was Dropped Down a Spiral* and sucked in all the water until she puked out her ass.

True story.

Dear Diary,

Rauan walks into a womb and orders a gallon of sin semen, then he decides he wants to write a sestina, Rauan wants his bad luck gone, a cup of Kidd Rock's semen costs a pretty poem, the sperm that endures the test of time, sperm like the human condition, the universal jizz trap, sperm like Shakespeare, in a park, in a slate garden sliding down the walls like worms.

"Lyte as a rock" as Lily would say, but Rauan doesn't give her a say, he corrects her spelling.

I make it a rule never to read sestinas with the word "sperm" in the title.

Rauan's mind as a collective sperm omelet, this is Rauan's brain on deprivation, this is what happened to Rauan's brain after snorting lexical repetition, it was a sin.

Rauan decides to get out more.

Rauan dating a neanderthal version of his college girlfriend, to prepare for his date he prepares to leave her because he's feeling nostalgic for an older revision.

Rauan dating a daughter of the patriarchy, don't worry she was adopted, daughters of the patriarchy are always adopted, to prepare for his date he writes an intensive haiku sequence considering limited space to infinite sperm in his man-book,

Rauan taking space, preparing a meal, preparing his vows, making his case.

Rauan isn't prepared for the real thing.

THE WOMB IS NOT A METAPHOR, YOU TREASONOUS TWAT.

A gallon of rules, a gallon of morals and violations, Rauan advertised as a destructive context, Rauan offered as the inevitable consequence of delusion, thousands of gallons of consequence spilling into the space referred to here as Rauan.

YOU DIDN'T HAPPEN, RAUAN.

But he's here nonetheless.

Dear Diary,

Today Lily and I flew over a beautiful swamp and in its water a swan tangled in its luscious green plants. This we viewed as the great pain festering in the foliage. The great pain who had it coming. We paid a lot for that house in the swamp with the view of the swan suffering, but we never stepped foot inside. We could have paid for a bedroom balcony overlooking a courtyard or private baths so nobody could see us when we peed. We could have stayed inside with the curtain drawn, lit candles and read poetry journals to one another. But we chose to board our hang gliders and get the big perspective.

Saw it all from up there.

We gasped when the swan gasped and we flew when the swan swallowed more swamp water.

This perspective was not as pleasurable as it sounds. Maybe it would be better if I trudged into the swamp and strangled the swan with my own hands? Lily suggested that I had more pressing needs to smother.

Lily authored a snuff list and seeks representation. She'd been destructively productive in her box.

Dear Diary,

Slots coming up Rauan, the high toll of touching Rauan's bare ass, the high toll touches, the high toll rings, touching Rauan's hideous mother's face, what a bitch for blocking his conception, what a bitch for inviting herself to our big night out, for spending our nickels, what a lovely face, what a wonderful shoe, what Rauan wants Rauan associates, this is an ass, this is a beast, she is your mother too.

Don't you want somebody to love?

Brand new shoes, shoes like a dyeable event, gray lace dress, fancy for Rauan, pushing the switch, Rauan takes a bath and wow, that's rich, that's bling to get you past the doorman, that's bling you can take to the sperm bank, if a uterus had a gatekeeper we'd be millionaires.

What a difference Rauan makes.

Difference in waking life, the main difference is stress, another difference is gender, and another is intent, that time Rauan called me a "nuclear retardant" because he wanted to see me cry.

He thought I forgot.

A face curled algorithm, inflammation, a strange strategy for a face, face like a wart, face as a weapon, facing the spray of spittle and salt and realizing it tickles.

The difference between archetypes and schedules.

Won't you need somebody to love?

The symbolism of the rotting face spirits and the paths introduced, hitting my face with my face, the difference between me and previous generations was that I touched his face like a recovered Kleenex in a winter coat's pocket, there to absorb as the parasite, happy, strong in the place that exists in the aftermath.

Rauan believes he exists to a mend a fence, smooth some ripples, make a bread pudding with scraps of bygones and foreskins that evolves into a rope bridge.

You better find somebody to love.

Swamps don't ripple and there is no fence because their boundaries never existed except in my darkest of hopes, the Rauan wants what the Rauan wants.

This can't end well.

A Contemplation

Rauan, who was never right, rains, and I'm wishing I would have checked the weather first.

Rauan, who was never subtle, rains and seeps through the crack that was too frightened to break any mother's back.

Rauan, who never owned property, rains, making houses cave, cave homes full of pantless men fighting Rauan's rain with the power pulsing between their echoing thighs.

Rauan, who weeps like a goosebump, rains on the worms, on the snakes and lizards who yip their postcards straight to a ribcage of lark.

Rauan, who knows my heart, rains on my heart, tells me he's peeing, tells me he could be persuaded to stop or he could continue and dissolve it all.

Dear Diary,

People with decomposing faces acting normally, like they're not from around here, like they have to graduate from someplace before their jaws collapse, how hideous this looks, trying to get home before I overheat, right away, dropped my jaw, I mean it, somebody help me find my jaw, I'm crumbling, crumbling, oh, what a kind bomb, what a kind bomb relieving me of the weight of my jaw.

 Taking the wrong way out, how to get out of the hole you've blown, on the wrong side and far from where I want to be, wrong direction, wrong road, misspelled and completely wrong, the wrong version, wrong part, wrong elevator, what he's saying is wrong, something wrong with his face, my logic rubbed him wrong.

 His face as the early stages of composition.

 Was I wrong to be bombed?

 Wrong again, wrote down the wrong number, paying attention in meaningful ways amounting to broader potholes, wrong side of the road, that spiral staircase is probably unsafe, wrong address, wrong contact, typing the password wrong, got my order wrong, wrong shoe, make a right, wrong turn, wrong lane, right back where I started, I said Andrew Carnegie built this, I meant Rauan shattered this and named it Rauanelot then changed it to Atlanrauan.

Rauan's name as the streaming piss from a fire hydrant's nightmares.

Rauan sinking all his names, sinking along the time span when I could distinguish one man from another by his name, these brand identities reflecting how he once wished to be reflected in our shields, so wrong, Rauan, trend transcendence isn't how you impress a busy mom, you're simply not a name she can trust.

You're not even a name she recognizes.

Recovered Memory

Milan was simply untenable. The Greek men just wouldn't take no for an answer and I would count the description of the entire experience as tiresome if I couldn't feel my uterus hemorrhaging every time a man approached to ask my name.

I walked faster, but my new pair of heels were a challenge. Comfortable, but so clumsy. No keeping an even stride for me. Not sure if anything was kept for me. But I did return to my rental unscathed and began to relax when the doorbell rang. There stood a Greek boy offering the gift of storage. Very sweet, but I told him he was young and should hold on to his gifts because one day he'd grow up and would need them himself. Frankly, I had little use for youth or sweetness.

Time passed, I think, and I don't know how, but the boy's feet were cut off. To be honest, it was appalling, but more appalling was the priority put on retrieving his feet. Everyone knew his feet were in a swamp, but the authorities slated the retrieval for later in the year when the weather was expected to improve.

Uncharacteristically, I felt responsible and decided to be the one to retrieve the boy's feet even though I was certainly no scuba expert. The experts told me not to worry, they'd handle it. But I insisted. I felt the boy deserved his feet now and to not have to wait until a hypothetical spring thaw. This responsibility forced me to swim through a series of underwater doors, no doubt a test to see if I could handle immersion into the swamp.

To the chagrin of the scuba divers, I passed, barely. They suited me up and allowed me to submerge myself into the swamp to retrieve the feet. Once underwater I couldn't hear anything, but was pretty sure the scuba divers on the surface were making fun of my breathing.

"Thar she blows a chunky feathered fish!"

Dear Diary,

Looking for the restroom, looking for some place unoccupied, claiming to be looking for a bell to ring, looking personable, looking for something fancier, overlooking plastic sheets, looking at the house when it looks like this, looking around at the many funny dog faces, gazing at Terrifyingly Handsome tethered to his water-logged corpse, plucking feathers for my pillow, looking at his highlights, wanting to stroke all 10 shades, wanting to forget that once I intentionally created him, wanting to look at his face rot differently.

He's looking forward to his leaving.

He's looking forward to a place where the women aren't so vocal and emaciated.

He's looking forward to his unknown like he'll be given a voice.

How funny my abandonment is to him, down here, looking, like a personal loss, like fermenting fruit in miniature parts, in a drawer, in a space right off the bedroom.

He's a corpse, snickering and freed, free to float away, fully believing he served his creator's purpose, believing he met his obligations, believing he's a good human being.

Fully believing that only the creator can be the monster, not considering the implication that brings to her creations.
I remind him that he's in a swamp, not a river.
The only place to go is down.

Dear Diary,

Oink-eye black, a snake swimming, a potential archetype, discovering one another's trickery, tiny green snakes with spots, trick types, spies pretending to be cops, honey doing the trick, a little device doing the trick, no treating, the banana as a very mean trick, the trick of loving him, tricking to love, never been mothered, trick window, tricky to play.

    Be careful he's a trickster.

    He's a Capricorn One with Patriarch Rising and yeah, he won, trick to give, pretend performance, pretend keys, pretending to celebrate Christmas with him, pretend shopping spree, pretend banking, pretend sleep, pretend attack, I don't see him, pretending to run, pretend brother, pretend Michael Jackson, pretend penis, pretend hug, pretending I'm OK, pretending I don't need to eat, pretending I never wanted to eat.

    The goddess pretends to cut her hand.

    She cuts the skunk and puts its blood in our space hero's drink, she's a spy pretending to be a Buddhist named Trixie.

    This poison brought to them by their conspiracies of need.

    They take it in.

    For the record.

Dear Diary,

Today's concern about the proper use of orbs and their many implications may not be a concern after all.
 Maybe the concern is being alone in a hotel room, waiting for the waiting to stop, maybe murder is the concern, maybe she'll be prosecuted for her crimes, maybe the death should be recreated in a bathtub, there might be concern as to whether a person can ever truly be dead, somebody take away her orb, tell her she can't participate in this expedition anymore, tell her she wasn't pulling her weight, tell her that we hate her so very bad.
 People done gone underground, people don't concern themselves with their litter cluttering the community, when we emerge from the underground the middle-aged woman points her gun at me, "be tougher," she says, "bad things happened down there for a reason and don't you forget that."
 Her new strength makes her the unpleasant, paranoid woman who is truly correct, tough to make out, pretty much tough shit, she doesn't need a bed to rest her head, she dreams in the tough language of advertisements, she barks a mean jingle when you touch her, you have to rewind really slow, it's a tough time getting to work, it's tough walking stairs in these sharpened sandals.

It's tough giving the message to hurry up and save the pooch, tougher when the job entails a feathered grimalkin.

I tell it to the tough guy plotting to fix things, the one who always has a tough time relaxing, he tells me he's tall, I tell him to stand up and prove it, I explain how it all went down, I tell him Rauan's gone rogue collecting innocent feet to clomp around, Rauan thinks if he can dive deep enough he can touch her, Rauan's returned to Middle Bombyonder with my identity and Tough Guy needs to bring him back to Upper Bombyonder because we need him to stay unconceived, I tell Tough Guy I don't care how, I can tell Tough Guy is not a happy excavator, he doesn't want to do this, he's neither a Christian nor a supporter of the death penalty and this seems like little more than necrodiving.

He's concerned about crossing boundaries, I tell him I understand that he needs to simmer down.

I tell him to move it.

I tell him to dig like its his own grave.

I tell him these corpses aren't for his sensual pleasure.

They're for mine.

Dear Diary,

Painting something blue, something fantastic and all encompassing like it came from a beak, can Rauan distinguish between the purples and blues?

Does Rauan know there's more to life than reds and browns?

Does it matter?

What I'm describing is the painted blue flesh of his death, it's coming, it's always coming, peck peck.

Rauan thinks because he's never been born he can't be killed.

I could kill him as easily as I gobble down this blue licorice, as quickly as I discard these cutouts and show offs, I could kill simultaneously as I lift weights while visualizing a yellowed wedding dress.

A blue bird drops a shatter striking its target, this eye patch makes my eyes blue, covered like a pink, parrot-faced cat, packed in a blue duffle bag.

Has that predatory owl been watching me the whole time?

Probably.

I tell her to go report back already to her astronaut-fellating goddess.

It's just not right, concrete roller rink where the tree used to be, weeping willow bombed like a blueberry pie cut out of a photograph, blue like slither, there must be more than one snake down the hole, spots and a goal slipped the mind, the honey in the hair combs turned bright, penetrating like a peeled banana.

Nobody seems impressed by creation anymore.

It's all "let's see what we can salvage from the rubble and what stories we can invent to put ourselves at ease and on a park bench plaque."

They forget when they change the future the past must correlate, when they changed Rauan, they changed the history of monetary abuses in these great pits.

They erased their own legacies.

Recovered Memory

My trailer graffitied but it was much worse than that. The animals inside hadn't behaved, they went positively wild. The leopard ate the caretaker and most of the cow. All that was left of Mizmoo was her head and shoulder, sounding so mellow, mooing on the floor, like she forgot a leopard gobbled her. Maybe she understood that her purpose was delicious.

All I found of the caretaker was his silent, severed foot.

Difficult to say if this was my fault, if the animals should have been fed, if it was my responsibility to feed them. Should I have separated them? Put up some kind of boundaries? I left them as they arrived. Who was I to implement a change in the order? I barely could make sense of the existing rules. Couldn't even be sure the leopard was the culprit, but the zebra hadn't appeared as a contender. It had to be the leopard, the zebra was inconsequential.

The scrawl on the outside of the trailer:

THE VICTIM IS
THE PERPETRATOR IS
THE VICTIM IS

THE CULPRIT IS
THE CASUALITY IS
THE FUSE AND
THE FUTURE
JUST A PAWN IN
THE END

An outfit calling itself "The Carries" claimed authorship and included an email address.

Clearly an attack on my feminism with bait for my reply.

I gave no reply nor showed any tears or concern. I walked away and when I returned much later all that remained were leather specks and bone splinters, piled like magic refried beans, like a pile of runny shit caught in a rainstorm.

Don't ever bring my feminism into question again, you psycho-cunted arsonists, I seethed to the specks and splinters, *else I'll rain down onto you the most terrible Twitter mob who will tweet your titties to crumbs.*

Unrecovered Memory

Who was Medusa speaking to when she said, "Unarmored as I am   you can / take my head for your fucking / chaste warrior shield"?

Athena? Perseus? Her mother? Was Medusa angry? Frightened? Was she just acting tough or did she really mean it? Mean what? What did she mean? Was she giving up? Resigned to her fate?

Perhaps I made a decision. Perhaps, as a two-time murderer as well as a hopeful future murderer, I couldn't be the victim. But why not be the monster and the hero? Perhaps a heroic monster? Terrible and brave and destructive. I'd start with vengeance. If I discovered somebody skull fucked Medusa, the proper response is to penetrate him with my ASS pencil. In this instance I'd make an exception to be a penetrator of a penetrator, on my grandmother's side. Knock this orb so far down his throat, he'd think his very own dead bird cried within him. He'd try to cough it up. Impossible as the weight of the orb sunk into his bowels.

What would Medusa do?

The great dingbat with / her shield of / cracked mirrors a / shard to be reckoned with!

Dear Rauan,

You don't want to hear about marriage, but you're going to get it, you're going to get insurance, you're going to start making sense, you're going to get the girl too, the power you're going to get is negligible, you're going to get married.

Soon.

No end to your noodle sampling, worried that you're creepily calm, presumably, second thoughts, you're a very old woman, Rauan, you think these are rental agents, they're marriage healers, they're going to expect you to do the laundry, they're not sure of your daughter's gender, she could be accepted as a boy, or accepted as an art form, or an acceptable body count, love is love, disappointment in a burst of light, every time you open your mouth its like a strobe light taking a shit in a bucket.

Living among towers and juice boxes, blended families, retelling this story feels over and agitated, like escaping from prison by letter bomb, what else escaped and expects to get caught?

You accepted before speaking, this unwritten manuscript already accepted for publication, you don't want to be accepted, you haven't accepted my friend request, wink, wave, you're such a sad faker, boo hoo, what's in your bio, veiled brother, what did you list as your location, work and education history, do you have a favorite television show, how many likes have you given and to what?

This wave knocks you down, if that wave comes you'll be dead, if this wave comes you'll be better off dead, you wouldn't recognize a wave if it fell from the sky and wiggled on your face, time to wave and drive off, I'll wave you through, don't acknowledge it, acknowledge you're missing, acknowledge this is a dare, I acknowledge family warfare exists, wave and smile, Rauan, turn on the camera and smile, you know how to dance, now freeze, now tell me, one more time, what are you doing here and what is it that you want?

Dear Diary,

Rauan mocking the border as his way to emerge.

I'm the border of Rauan, I draw the lines.

Rundown Rauan who hasn't been updated, surreal and awful Rauan full of purples and blues, moving towards a new Cornish, not for future benefit, but for the benefit of a revival, Rauan as a dead language, traveling to a place called His before we got called away to Algebra, a few yards into the border we reach the town of Bird Call, neighboring the Decapital.

At this point I'm considering giving up, we keep driving south but can't get past the town of Worm, it's everywhere and it's deep and penetrating.

Shouldn't have let Rauan drive.

Shouldn't have called Rauan a cock deathmaster.

I delete Rauan and he agrees to counseling, meets with a raccoon-faced dragon called Exterminator, they have a productive talk.

This process refer to itself as psychic intertextuality.

Is Rauan more powerful unconceived or dead? There's always a speck of future possibility for a later date for the unconceived. Better luck next time.

But for the dead there is the potential for legacy.

For the historian, Rauan has many non-existing meanings, for the stylish he's an allusion to the mandrake, hipsters name their death erections after him, Rauan as an image that only makes sense in the dark of borderline knowledge.

For an archaeologist, Rauan derives meaning for my benefit, my notion that he's a code to be cracked into usable quotes for the benefit of the middle classes, as an archaeologist, he fits into my final form to comprehend the allusions of deficiency, though generally he simply refers to users who use his name as a theory to be alluded to in a future text.

Scuba divers believed the Rauanelk to be extinct for a thousand years. Beliefs are limited to what can be proven and it was never proven that Rauanelks lived underwater. There were sightings, which in the end, were always attributed to excessively hairy, armored mermen.

Historians found no written, oral or visual records of any Rauan or Rauanelk. Historians believe him to be neither fact nor myth. Historians simply don't believe in the existence, nor the imaginative possibility, of Rauan.

Dear Diary,

We work the whack seam together, stitching up to those indulgent ambitions, the factory women make fun of us, years to work through this dust cloud just to get to a new dust cloud, I wear my hair however I like, ten flattering styles to choose from and I picked them all, everything works with an open mind.

Make a U-turn to work, so much work getting the tape to adhere to something stable, work interfering with work, working a scammy sales job, working nights during the day, discussing work, kitchen work, don't give specifics, something specific, looking for a specific mummy named "Carry," they're all named Carry, making a more specific search party, I plan on blowing up something that doesn't want to be blown, something that's already blown, something that doesn't know it's been blown countless times before and is susceptible to more.

I plan to kill some texts and breaths, gamble, write a book without periods, raze the rubble, smite it, blank it, write it out, white it out, go back to Europe on an inflatable raft, and fuck my great great great great great great grandfather into a state of vegetation, then go find my my great great great great great great grandmother and tell her nothing personal.

Every mother restored to what never existed, every brother who never was, but should have, will be, or won't.

I was never here, have never met myself, there is no place where I lived, I came from down nowhere, without work history, experienced in nothing tangible.

Recovered Memory

On this meeting with this particular ancestor named Carry, I was surprised by her mask and its thickness. Hardly a way in or out. Not at all clownish but with brown scales, leather and bolts.

How strange to hear her speak through the clamp for a mouth and to be seen through her single, tiny eyehole. How muffled her words sounded through the barriers. How uncomfortable to know she cried behind that foulness not because it was foul, but for the sake of her brother, an accused molester of the vulnerable.

Trouble with the law. There's always so much trouble with laws for this family.

Who did this to you?

"The women and children, like they always do, their cruel, perverted imaginations that they just can't keep to themselves. They have to share their inventions, and share for years, they whisper and then they group together and then they testify and allow it all to go down as record. They perverted it all, smote his perfect legacy."

No, I mean who put that mask on you? Why are you still wearing it? What is behind it?

"My brother placed it on me, for my salvation. He's my protector. There are so many terrible women and children spouting their wretched tales, repeating and publicizing. They let nothing go! What lies behind this mask hasn't yet been penetrated. So little left that hasn't been penetrated. My face is one of the last pure bastions."

You can hardly see or speak through that mask and it smells like your skin is decaying under there.

"Yes, the decay keeps me safe. Frightens away the children and many of the women too. No one is going to scavenge me for their depraved narratives. Forever I remain unmolested."

But her corpsed-face remained unmolested no longer.

Because now I was there, smelling it, imagining its appearance, inventing my memories.

Dear Diary,

How do I keep ending at Rauan?
    Thwarted words lead the aborted, obstruction creates the unconceived.
    Rauan stuns with every wardrobe change, Rauan stuns in elaborate gold, stuns with cleavage and bulge, stuns in his sheer costume, stuns in statement jewelry, stunned by a versatile poopshute, stunned with desire for Mother.
    To get access one must be willing to walk to the end of Rauan, this end pretty empty, this end pretty near, Rauan as a high-end condo, not affordable, this end feels totally different, at this end Rauan says he's sorry but he can't let me through and that's OK, salvation versus birthright, at the end it's only Rauan, no refund.
    It's difficult to explain.
    Difficult to talk one's visions, difficult to say, sending a difficult child away, Rauan and the difficulty of crossing children, a difficult life, difficult circumstances, but I'm doing it, taking off Rauan's fancy lace dress, he wears it on the inside, on this inside a beaver looks alive, on that inside a cactus grows, my inside is a little bit pleased now that it can't escape, a little bit pleased there might be an end.

Going inside to explain Rauan to Rauan.

Hurts on top of all these brass shattered orbs, this orb connected to that piece, the struggle of conversation pieces, stringing a piece for Rauan, this piece makes holes, this piece partially eaten, the first piece, feminine, the second, Rauan and the third, the low bridge to a nuclear rhyming reactor.

A lot of pieces, remembering Rauan, piece by piece, on further inspection he's missing, he's riding on a winged horse, nobody files a missing persons report because he's hiding in my intestines and won't get very far.

Rauan as the best story every written.

Rauan as a tragedy measured in ferret pelts.

Best take advantage of his dress, doing my best to wish him the best, wish this part was really a skit with a clapping audience, wish I knew how we got these tumors, wish someone would teach me something about birds, how to understand their signals, how to distinguish a bird from a feline.

I don't understand why everywhere I go is Rauan, I don't understand why nobody understands, what does Rauan symbolize, what is the meaning of a place called Rauan?

The worst part of Rauan filled with the worst people, this place takes people from their bodies and uses their bodies, this place humps corpses for sport, or knowledge, or love, what a scam finding value in people, well sometimes you have to scam to live, so we hook up people watching videos to the internet, we hook animals up to the people and this becomes a really popular video, people always misunderstand, people want to hurry up and get this over with, rush and shush, boomba.

I keep yelling *occupied* until Rauan understands and stops banging on the stall, he could climb out, he could climb over and jump down into his dangerous neighborhood to be eaten by alligators, he could climb the ladder and lose his breath, he could climb to the next level but oh he says it's too difficult, he could climb out the window, he throws my coffee cup at the window, he could climb up the staircase and panic if it were not for these tricky walls, he could climb outside but that's difficult and scary too.

    Rauan climbs back into his dress and is greeted by two snakes, one blue, the other red, Rauan must choose which snake will bite his face off.

    He doesn't need his old face, I made him new faces, one is a blue parrot face that looks a lot like a lizard crossed with a cat, the other, inflamed and decomposed, with rotting horses strewn about, the one I'm urged to lick.

    Rauan, pick the red snake and see how deep your gown goes!

Note from a Carry

Beware of the panic.
The suspicious monster
pretending to fight.
In this dimension you're
capable of fighting
pretty much everything that
confronts you but
how do you fight the
machine attached at
your temples?
The cops trace the panic and
oh fuck
THE PANIC IS COMING FROM
INSIDE THE NARRATIVE.

Signed,
C

Recovered Memory

Maybe the snake wasn't a snake but a person, maybe, perhaps, possibly, but to me it looked like a giant white snake so there was nothing else to do but cut its head off. I couldn't get the saw all the way through and then the altar caught on fire and then who knows what happened to the snake. It was gone.

Most of the pages of my father's bible incinerated, but two tiny leather-bound volumes remained unscathed, filled with poems written from the fragments of older poems eaten and shat.

Since I failed at my snake killing, my new task became rewriting those post-shat texts. The problem with recovery is that when you don't go very far from where you were born, you shit and piss where you live, the same place where your parents, and their parents shat and pissed and so on. Meaning you're swallowing the same ancient, recycled shit and piss that seeped into the wells that all the generations drank before you. Pretty sure I didn't need to drink from the water, that shit was already in my blood.

Original pickled veins.

Or maybe that wasn't my problem. Maybe the problem was my murderous impotence. Or maybe the problem was seeking solutions through killing. All these corpses brought a great deal of appropriated pickles. And snakes. And penises.

The phallus quandary?

The fallacy of phalluses?

Talk about distractions. When you added it all up, these penises didn't amount to much.

Recovered Memory

Clearly I didn't know what I was doing because I lingered. Lingered too long over short lines and sped through the longer passages. Patience wasn't my virtue. There was no virtue. Just a steady plate of irritability. No, that's taste, I'm talking about sight. What I could see was a lot like touch, I could feel what I tasted. My passage through the hole included a scuba diver who said it didn't get much deeper than this. Imagined a time out of my depth, not that I was sure of my potential for depth. Had I potential? Getting close was practically a letdown. Was that really all it was?

I remember the advice: "Don't slink around it, sink into it, like a rock encased in cement paying big bucks for nibbles from high-class fishes."

I remember the slow movement through the hole many years long followed by the crash and the resulting outburst.

I don't remember ever reaching another opening or an end. Maybe the opening collapsed. Maybe that wasn't it. Maybe it wasn't anything. Maybe there's nothing to get or miss. Maybe there never was an opening. Maybe there was no escape.

The _____ at the end of the tunnel never reached is a blank I do not possess.

Recovered Memory

The security guard centered the rose within the chalk outline. He went on and on how the woman in question once owned the most magnificent rose so fresh it bloomed sparks of Medusa before she was cursed for her vulnerability. Until the mother got sick of the rose and flushed it. Or until the father crushed it into a bookmark to mark his spot. Nobody tried to stop the mother. Nobody thought the father outside his right. In short, nobody stepped up for the rose. Nobody moved or spoke or said, "Hey, something falling from the sky is about to crush a rose."

    Got the feeling this was a vital clue but didn't understand and quickly lost patience. I knew about snakes and worms and shields and corpses, the vomit, the bird, the girl, the donkey, the orb, the pencil and its many penetrations, the masks, the lizards, there were so many pieces and a rose didn't seem a particularly relevant or interesting addition to the mix. It seemed all rather high school and cliché.

    Maybe I gave up.

    Maybe I lost its meaning.

    I tended a rose bush once, never bloomed and I never bothered anyone with its tales. Red Rose, Axl Rose, a luxury of roses, the rise of bombs, the rose of verse, a rose for Rauan, a rose by any other name, rose wrist corsage, roses for sale, roses for the corpses, petals like feathers, rose-flowered eyes, rose-colored impotence.

    I recorded none of it.
    Kept it all to myself.

Recovered Memory

We asked the toddler, why us? What are we supposed to do? Where are we supposed to be digging? The obvious questions, the question already asked, Rauan covers his ears in anticipation of the terrible sound, the pain demanding protection from what's about to pierce its ears.

Was it time to tell everyone that we're two of the hundred to change the world?

We were the 2% and our impotence astounded the filthy percent.

As contributors to the scramble, before we entered the massive tree trunk we asked it not to poison us. Rauan thought this might be the Tree of Life. But I knew it wasn't. I recognized the Rape Tree from its branches from which hung a white bull, a swan, a dagger in a heart, fresh foreskins, tongues, swallows, nightingales, bangbots, runes, seeds, torches, ignored prophecies, decapitations and a lot of asking-for-it masks.

But then I thought more about it, wasn't the Rape Tree what gave birth to continents?

Eventually we agreed, both of us were right, the Rape Tree is the Tree of Life. Same thing. You have to take and destroy to create something new, so it can grow up to take and destroy or be taken and destroyed. If something isn't being taken so it can be destroyed, nothing's happening.

Rauan wore a mask so to not breathe in the alien. The alien was not a toddler, the toddler was the alien. The toddler was the blue-faced girl as a toddler, not a bird, the blue girl sounded like a computer. Rauan beeped but she still came through sounding like a crazy coincidence. She could sound out so many of the words. We were all very proud, she sounded fabulous, like a weed named Yankee Doodle Rauan. We all agreed to live in sound. Except humming Rauan, he's never agreed. He never had an opportunity to agree.

In this clear water we called the floating plants Germanic Rauan because let me pee on your feet and cure that rash already.

What a system. I rewrote Rauan so he never dropped the baby from the donkey, I rewrote Rauan to suck sound. I rewrote Rauan to possess a secret change slot of his very own with the option to decide whether he'd accept your change. I rewrote *The Girl With the Dragon Tattoo* and made it all about Rauan sucking Pegasus's terrifying shriek.

I renamed it *The Rauan with the Pegasus Sound*, sounding familiar, but totally unique.

Unrecovered Memories

I don't remember who spoke the name claiming it was mine but I remember my refusal.

Who can say how large a personal space one is morally expected to give and to receive.

I don't remember the taste of fish, but I suppose it doesn't taste too different than swan or snake or worm or ferret.

I don't remember any of the questions regarding the powers of abuse, but I do remember reading the answers in the *Foreskinned Manifesto*.

I don't remember the small things in which a clue to a name may burrow.

I don't remember any reasons, the particular circumstances or what was once the perceived ideal, all unrecognizable goals, all closures, tricks of smoke and dragon tears.

I don't remember what was brought to light and what was scrambled with the eggs on drugs or if I agreed to the importance of breakfast.

I don't remember the stilted chants we practiced every day but I remember being visited by something like a wraith offering an invitation to flee the bothersome, an invitation in the form of a bed.

Dear Diary,

We walk as we talk, limp and dragged, it grows very dim, a sparse path with fewer books, have you seen Rauan kicking the lights, frustrated they're not shining enough light on him?

Have you seen Rauan holding his breath like he could commit suicide?

Have you seen Rauan try to muscle like a big man?

Have you seen Rauan?

In a bathroom, is he looking for something, something personal, does he find relief?

Would he recognize relief?

Glancing Rauan, this place isn't as private as he'd like, this is a busy town, this looks bad, this looks like a bald man through a window hanging himself with Beatles lyrics, all he needs is love (from a mother), this is where Rauan spends his nights, all he needs is a corporeal form, this is a bad generation full of robot limbs and heads, all he needs is a future, something's poisoned, a poison to improve sexuality, a poison to get you a date, a poison to read your aura, the champagne of poison bursts across a thousand reptilian tongues.

Does Rauan drink the poison?

Does Rauan suck off the bomb?

No, Rauan suffers through passive meat, suffers a poisoned convenience of corner store doughnuts, Rauan suffers a psychic jealousy of logic, a logic that can't be swayed by logic, the logic of orphaned body bags, of lost parts insisting they're not lost but wandering, what exactly do they suppose they're not missing?

The rubbed logic of a conversation unlikely to go how you would hope, one becomes two, two becomes three, three becomes the one called Rauan.

Dear Diary,

Hilarious songs on the fly sung by Rauan, the hilarious trail of slugs leading to Rauan, yes with a zipper going up his ass, yes with a dewey decimal, yes I heard of Rauan, I heard he wanted to be heard, I heard he wanted to be somebody, I don't buy it, I heard she left him unused, I heard she left him wanting something, anything, saying yes to Rauan might lead to something hilariously creepy, yes banana, yes tighty-whitey, he's a creeper, yes buy it, someone's dick is breaking, yes really.

    Really getting off this stick, Rauan investing in real deal real estate above the flood plain, the real prisoner escapes, the real prisoner wakes up as a beautiful woman, possibly a movie star with champagne expectations and a caviar complex, the real woman intoxicated, real woman as mostly botox and snot, when I say that's snot funny, it really isn't.

    Real messages meant only for Rauan, sorry, Rauan can't hear you because there's a sock monkey's dick in his ear, clogged with sock monkey dick snot, rejecting Rauan because he isn't a real word, he's an invention of a name which technically makes him nameless, not that he'd ever admit that, not that he'd ever give up his imaginary name, not that he'd willingly give up his place among the placeless.

Rauan's desire for a maternal bond really isn't my thing, mansplaining motherhood to Rauan, life-like caregivers cobbled together with plaque, Rauan's real hair is an orange wig because hair can't sprout from nowhere, Rauan announces he wants to spend the day with real people, real relatable people named Trampled and Busted Up.

Rauan reinvents himself as the real world master.

Rauan trumps us all, Rauan's real name is Busta Enzyme.

Rauan goes really far back in time to teach primitive women how to assert themselves, Rauan imagines labias like diamonds, jackpot uteruses, Rauan invents a poetic form that expresses the beauty of vaginas in spite of their rhinestoned agony coining the term Vaghazal for posterity.

Rauan makes rape fake, Rauan makes it safe for primitive women and now primitive women don't have to worry how to survive, all primitive women need to do now is focus on their children, hairdos and shoe collections, no threat here, no siree, primitive women never had it so good!

Rauan retunes the archetypal mother.

Rauan swipes her teeth and replaces her fillings.

Rauan polishes his vagina dentate charm bracelet with hope for a new possibility.

Rauan becomes the Magical Rauan possessing special insights and mystical powers, so patient and wise, so self-sacrificing, he becomes the key to primitive women's redemption, Rauan becomes an American tradition like the Noble Rauan and Rauan Savage.

Rauan changes the timeline by simply appearing to aid and enlighten primitive women, Rauan's real name is now Luke Twatblocker, Rauan saves us so we never needed a savior, Rauan saves us so we never needed him, Rauan who made it so that for me to still exist, he couldn't happen, for real this time.

Rauan really never happened because he can't be infantilized.

Rauan can never be an infant because he's never gotten close to conception.

Rauan's charm bracelet crumbles.

Her teeth reemerge, sharper, with more puncture than before Rauan changed the timeline.

Rauan's desire for a maternal bond makes the world worse.

I wouldn't touch Rauan with a ten-foot sock monkey, I wouldn't touch Rauan because there's nothing there, he accepts his new challenge and saves a dog's life, save your energy, save this plot twist for your memoir, save it for another day, save it for your hope chest.

Maybe Rauan can be fixed, maybe Rauan can save us from birthing dead vomit birds in the near future, even with all the changes we're still filled with all these dead birds, hindsight did not give Rauan the ability to address the dead birds or the kind bomb, hindsight offers no gifts to Rauan, hindsight mocks Rauan's creeping determinism, hindsight takes an enormous shit on his historical reconstruction and rubs his face in it.

Rauan changes nothing.

Rauan couldn't even save the basement carpet after the flood, Rauan's life is a hole in the bucket, Rauan's gift cards don't ring up, Rauan as a useless freebie, nobody inscribes a bench with the name of an unnecessary hero.

What do we recall?

When do we want to recall it?

Note from a Carry

To assist the ordered
kindred fluster
named as the extinct and blessed
we sketch a timeline
to offer emphasis
to these layers of humanity
and suggest a point of
view to be confronted and
revised at a later
time by future descendants
with their need to
reshape the line into a
different form.

The rest we ignore.

Signed,
C

Dear Diary,

We would have walked the swamp with our ears and listened with our toes, but this isn't about what we could have done when we were younger, this is what can we do now, at this blurred point, atop this upside-down, pointed, tin-foiled hat we float like a raft tracking bomb robbers who we can't agree on whether to domesticate or slaughter.

    We can't change the future, only the past with our orbs and pencils.

    We can thread the needle, put it through one ear and out the other, we can coax out what's inside, we can do a good job, we can insert ear socks full of spiders, cats and listen for prey, we can trim the ear hair before we work the bookfair, still, we hear what we want to hear until we hear the bait that gobbles what needs to go away.

    I take Rauan to the store, I wait in the car, I take Rauan to the titty club, I wait in the car, I take him wherever he asks while I wait in the car but I can't take Rauan seriously.

    Sock-monkeys mugging Rauan of his many hopes and wants, Rauan yelling "fuck you in the ass," sock-monkeys fucking Rauan in his ear, this is what it sounds like when Rauan, being fucked in the ear by Sock-Mommy, cries, deeply troubled

Sock-Mommy with a clear meanness directed at his needs, Rauan sharing this experience on Facebook, Rauan writing a very sad poem on a sock, wanting me to feel what he feels.

I say, *just a little, please.*

Wearing good socks in borrowed shoes, my heart is a bowling alley, Rauan's soul is the ball's finger holes, I'm poking Rauan's soul on a Saturday afternoon in between building and Instagramming my memorial sausage castle.

Somebody needs to ensure the legacy.

Anybody?

Rauan tells me walking in filthy socks is simply not becoming of a princess, tells me princesses shouldn't smell like breakfast meat, Rauan tells me I should backtrack towards the swamp to wash it all away, Rauan tells me I really hurt his feelings, Rauan tells me to get out and start walking, Rauan tells me to squat over a burning bush and see what that feels like.

Then he tells me don't do it.

Rauan says next time get the black tuxedo, be my own damn man.

When Rauan and I fish, we cast like we're bowling, we're heavy like that, we sink far past Pompeii, our next cast our promised trophy, after that it's all characters, a predominately stained cast, stained like glass, stained like when we pee ourselves, stained like scorched genitals, stained like the unwalkable swamp that wants to bury us like forgotten milk teeth, stains like corpses of rude teenagers, stains like a boy crawling on the swamp floor digging for his sea-donkey.

One mucked-up, neglected sea-donkey.

Recovered Memory

I stepped through the door leading to the alley. The kind of alley where back in the day, when a hero is a helpless child, he's allowed to watch his parents be murdered right before his very eyes. Statistics show these are exactly the sort of events children block from their memories. Statistics show repression creates unintended consequences. Statistics show that orphans are the saddest creatures. Statistics show that these are the events ripe for revision.

Statistics put me in the middle of a bald-man duel.

One bald man wore an argyle sweater vest, the other had a reptile poking from the crown of his skull. One time my father had a sweater vest so I knew not to look. One time my father was possessed by a reptilian alien so I knew not to get close.

The duel was over quickly. A bald man died. A bald man was the victor.

Unconsciously I stroked the dead man's head knowing there must have been relations a long time ago. His corpse glowed a pregnant pox I hadn't cared to remember until this death and once I did care, I still couldn't remember. Statistics demonstrate memories get remembered one way or another in a suitable-for-framing fashion.

Statistics demonstrate tragic events to be game changers, if we replaced the term "human beings" with "players" or "avatars."

At Chalet Ice N Elk we prepared for the invasion. Then they got my father and we were leaderless. Statistics prove that only assbeasts are capable of leadership and we were fresh out. We called Mom. She screamed over the phone that she couldn't help it if our reptilian failure of a father died and besides, she already did her time and was now a free agent fielding considerably better offers.

So we embraced our new world order by adapting our lives to fit into alien society. All we could do to survive.

We embraced our new world order?

Struggling to remember the embrace.

We must have. We're still here.

Dear Diary,

The womanly book you only read when drinking at a party, trying to act busy, not awkward, an obelisk with the bust of a man as his tie flaps over his shoulder, maps showing the location of documentation, maps showing the hiding places of corpses and the closest corresponding shovels and this may get me arrested, this hiding in the toilet stalls of men.

An emergency of men.

This is the mouth I kissed my mother with, from the mouths of meatballs, kisses for the sausage eater, water fills a mouth and we all hope it's not piss, or at least that's the point of view of the tape placed over a kidnapped woman's mouth.

Children's mouths as offense, the unforgiveness of alligators and the consequences of snapping, his mustache dissolving into my chaste kiss, every time he loses a tooth it falls from my mouth, when you fail to document the mouth there is no map to the tongue, all specks lost, smoke in my mouth, all part of my act, every time I use my mouth it's an act in tragedy.

This mouth brought to you by the letter triangle.

Imaginary games of sound and shape, a mint in my mouth and a taste of future mustaches dissolving, the spider web as the mouth's veil, spinning a dramatic gag.

Certainly not a style everyone pulls off.

Dear Diary,

Really well put highlights, wild, famous and disconnected, shampoo experiment, volunteer rinse, adjusted stress tress, additional trim, sideburned private landing strip, thick ribbon strung, shaved orange wig, figuring out the giant bath, hair burning in a glass dutch oven.

Geometric bush-maze pattern—the new rage, find your self before you shill yourself before your self finds you infested with lice and tells the entire class, singled and shamed again.

Crones silvered to tarnish, clips among peeking roots, hair dunk, everywhere dog fur and vacuum, smooth snake shooter repurposed into a thong, permanent surprise, mustached roots, curling ringlets of wealth, defused donation bag, handsome locks resisting straightening.

I pee myself a little, I squat, it burns.

Psychic jealousy, knife-pressed conditioner, intense wastrel treatment, blonde-poured bleach, stuck engagement and a whole lot of toner, better bald rocker, salon scavenger, hairdone slop, sale ribbon, flat approach, crushed penis accessory, covert wet look, working afro, canned heavy heat, tubed devil horn, receding motherline, discouraged towel dry, blacker celebration, curly queued intention.

50 Hairstyles for Medusa-American Hair

Honey-mustard hairspray, more fish oil for the finish, more points, woken by a new face, grease rinse, greased reunion, earwax on the needle and I did a really good job punching that hole, I can see right through it, I can leave my hair wet and air dry, I'm a woman, long hair, breasts, see, woman, hole puncher, petting men like squirrels.

Kinky Joaquin Phoenix braids, shoebox full of bikini hair clippers, pick-up truck with a mattress where the engine should be, the world runs how the world runs.

Hairblown interpretation, declined.

It's a cash economy out there.

Vroom. Boomba and beyond.

Recovered Memory

Back in the waiting room I remembered reading about it before, a squirrel exploded into foam at this very dentist's office. Back then I was so sensitive, all of my cavities were genetic. Felt hideous with my long list of damages: UVed skin, yellowed teeth, bloodied gums, long history of grinding... when the dentist left my retainer on the toilet for me to retrieve all I saw was rhinoceros feet.

All I felt was foam curdling in my veins.

She brought and left me here, I thought. Stuck among the out-dated magazines until I got around to coughing up a dead bird to pay the bill.

Text from Lily to Rauan

LilyInABox: You can't be an alpha w/o a corporeal dick, you'll never be anything more than a torn page. #TrumpedAgainDawg.

Recovered Memory

A woman and her dingbat stuck in a ditch. The snowstorm came with its snowhands pushing a big wheel up the hill to roll down and free them. Maybe everyone worried about the weather when they didn't need to. Maybe the safest place during a snowstorm was buried in a ditch because you can't fight what's hard-wired.

Or maybe it's the least safe. Maybe the ditch filled with snow, then gravel, the heaviness, then salt and woman and her dingbat dissolve before Spring thaw.

On the other hand, what's outside the ditch?

The unknown. Uncertainty. No doubt dangerous men and scheming women humping things that haven't moved in years.

As if fleeing a ditch would provide any cover. As if a single wheel could be a roof for a woman and her dingbat. As if a snowstorm could be its own solution to the terror it creates.

A woman and her dingbat stayed stuck in a ditch.

In terror, huddling into a more comfortable terror.

But where did they pee?

Recovered Memory

As we lay in bed together my lizard dragged his long gaze across my recollection. My lizard the lover, the iguana, the prickly vulcan, the seizure delivered by butterfly. This widespread affair no one prepared to fight.

We prepared for other events. We prepared for traveling and camping, duffle bags tagged and zipped, ready for flight. We prepared hiding places for when the authority invaded to confiscate our pipes and pills. We dug bomb shelters, practiced drills, stocked gas masks.

Aside from some adequate meals, my preparations amounted to crumbled toys. The lizard came and I took him to my bed without inspecting his tongue or demanding his name.

Because he said I couldn't pronounce it and because I took him at his tongue.

The lizard kissed me with his mouth full of gears and robotics ready to collect and compute all the violent data with dates. Crumbs on the bedspread. Crumbs on the floor. Scraps. Morsels. Splinters. Bits.

Seeds.
Specimens.
Relics.
Impulses.

Letter from Lily,

That sudden shimmering body, caked with scales and this hot-ass clap scales the bleachers of your tunneled mind. I get it. He leans younger than he looks. Cold blooded and probably doesn't hug because what rhymes with hug overwhelms the averages. Give it a try and see what comes of this reptilian lover. What is left for him to damage? What haven't you broken? Or allowed to be broken? Or declined to repair when given the resources? Nothing will come of it, you heard it here first, but at least he's not a meat swan or an unconceived brother. I'm fresh out of resistance. I'm concerned I won't use what little air is left in this box trying to get through to you.

    But I'll say this, resting your wronged head on Rauan's ceremonial knee is beyond questionable, it's doom-inducing. Correct him and he says OK, install some reptilian blockers, like gerbils on wheels, now he's in charge of the whole damn wheel with his wallet riding on its fortune. The steering wheel fashioned into goose contraptions pulled from the hearts of men doing construction. It's embarrassing like roulette, the wheel of curing, riding the ferris wheel of limited amounts, brakeless.

    We suffer because we are vulnerable to suffering.

Rauan bitching about the care he's receiving yet keeps seeking. That's the definition of ferrets running the attic.

She doesn't care that his mommy issues take him away from his celestial pageant. Doesn't care one bit. She's not bothered. She says fate takes care of them all eventually like a burnt flat cake suitable for penis wrapping or worm nesting. She's taking care of her monsters not the pets. She's attached values and uses. She cares with a pink Care Bear blanket stuffed with bloodworms and needs all your possessions to support this caring because caring is expensive. There's a psychiatric spa that does a good job taking care of its people. That's where you should take Rauan. Have him fill out forms and give him a mami-pedi made for walking. Tell him it's for his health.

Truly,
Lily

Vague Memory

As a superhero, I found myself, countless times, in a stadium about to blow. All sorts of villains in those days with all sorts of names and compositions. Once I fought a gelatinous monster in the bottom of a stairwell. Destroyed it by running through it. Then it regenerated and that's the part of the memory I don't remember. Did or didn't I save the stadium? Did I survive? What was I wearing? Did I run fast? Was I brave? Did the gelatin threaten to return? Was I forgiven? Was I forgotten? Was the gelatin once on the side of good? If so, what turned the gelatin? Could the gelatin still be redeemed?

Was gelatin truly comprised of skin and crushed bones? How was that not monstrous? Who invented that recycling program? Talk about maternal revisionism. Yes, that's something I'd like to talk about.

When there's time.

Were there any other superheroes fighting on my side? Why did it always feel like such a solitary endeavor?

Why did this mask itch so much and what smelled so foul?

What was I breathing in?

Recovered Memory

Never forgot sexting the monstrous faces of butter, but for a long while I did forget the bloodied whales pulling themselves out of the river, beaching themselves on the road like a bloodworm tossed in a bowl of pasta.

We maneuvered around their bloated corpses like an art form. Those whales and their tired, flabby arms made us sick in all kinds of ways. Was it death or escape they crawled toward? Or did they just wish to be dicks and fuck up traffic?

If I had a toilet big enough, I'd have flushed them all.

To avoid a whale, a big truck full of men swerved and rolled over. An impatient motorist hit-and-ran the truck and the inevitable cop chase ensued. Some lady stood in the middle-of-the-road yelling at the cops.

I yelled, *Hey lady, you're a dingbat.*

She yelled back "How am I a dingbat?" and I yelled *Look around you, these are extreme days. Pick a side and get out of the way, wolves are coming for the blubber! They'll come for you too.*

Until that moment, I always hated the police, but with all the whales and the abandonment of the overturned truck the world seemed different, harder and more putrid. Something expired and the soft and foamy stopped doing it for me.

I wanted those pics to stop popping up on my cell. I needed the beeping to stop.

Dear Diary,

Chained to a large bird, this bird gets more water than me, pissing off the bird, bombing the bird, a bird flying into the audience, we all clap, two birds in the nest, the blue bird lying near a bush, wondering if the bird is going to use the bush as a bathroom, wondering how clean can this floor really be?

When I drop my doughnut, I think real hard before picking it up and eating it.

Wallowing in the dead bird is vomit, my shoes sink deeper and browner.

A swallow whole, huge bird made of wave, a one-time catch, a tempest, doves so close together they're practically connected.

Look, love doves.

No, bulimic vultures stuffed with laxatives.

Something is going to blow and it will certainly be foul.

Reviving the individually wrapped birds, turtles on alert, the pornographer with a large stick and bird of prey, the owl and the strange bird, bird-like critter in the lock.

It's like you can't offend people anymore.

A bird feeder rejected for not being the real world.

A very special birdcage, or a totem on a high pole, mythical confusion, owl as Easter chick, low hanging owl pendant, the owl from the ritual strikes.

She's not deformed, she's an owl.

She's not obsolete, she's a dodo.

She's not a mother, she's an ostrich.

Swinging under the headless ostrich tree, handheld goose contraption, goosenecks smeared with some high-grade shit, a less expensive ducky, the fatwa of rubber duckies, shivery yellow duckies offering no warmth, floating with personal menace.

It's not a swamp, it's a Jacuzzi and nobody ever got pregnant in a Jacuzzi.

A turtle, a salamander and a duck go into a grocery store and eat watermelon. They spit the seeds into a belly of vomit.

Dear Diary,

Suspending the olden times until further review, at times a destructive parent, at times a clogged drain, at times a promise collage, someday I'll sit down and figure this out, cross my bird cage, time for the tour, limited time for information, a few times is enough, having a tough time with the little ball, tight on time, time to put on my big-girl pants, welcome to the jungle, you're gonna cry, over our time, this time impossible, wasting crime against oh the humanity.

Time crawling past the fish crawling towards the soldier crawling, calling for his mommy and hurry up and die already.

Not spending enough time with Rauan, he complains, biding our time at Home Depot, he wants to buy buckets and perform a maternal bailout, maybe another time, killing time at the airport, time on my stained hands, guessing the time of storms, various competing times, donating time, all this time growing willow just to watch it wilt, the time of passing us by, what a meaningful pipequest he's smoking, stinking up the place.

This time we're taking a boat straight to the beginning, I fall asleep, I wake up, roll over into a puddle of swamp pee where Rauan was supposed to be.

But there's more than one beginning, and Rauan's not present at this beginning, we can't find one another.

Heading towards a low bridge, heading towards a war to taunt the skirmish between the radar, maybe I'm a spy sent to kill a man, maybe he's supposed to kill me, maybe we'll fall in love, no, our mission, that we chose to accept, eliminate everything the other loves before the other eliminates you.

The novelty of boats, a hotel that looks like a boat, chairs floating like boats, these rapids don't know the meaning of raging, these rapids don't deserve their name, these rapids are temporary, they don't last long enough for a name, I'm going to forget them all in a heartbeat and laugh about it later.

Tinsel on the water, tinsel on their legs, tinsel like alligators, tinsel like a progressive bend, raft like garbage, happy to dock, rigid in the speedboat, tinsel like kool-aid mouthprints on a very cheap book, rhinestones as a tall girl with natural orange hair, rhinestones as eyes sparkling out far enough to blind.

It's raining tinsel.
HALLELUJAH!
It's raining tinsel.
Take cover, my lovesucked Rauan.

Farewell to Diary Entries

Goodbye doors, goodbye cratered floors, down the walk-up, goodbye and driving away, waving to parents as we exit, really good times, this might be goodbye, dying and posting farewell notes on my Facebook wall, collecting numerous likes, my most popular wall post of all time and now I have the klout.

Goodbye to the parade of princes and their well-grounded, minced words.

Well, I need a few more minutes, I thought I wanted to leave, but haven't thought where to exist next, now that I said I'm leaving, I'm receiving a great deal of positive affirmation.

It's nice to be liked.

Yet troubling that no one asks me to stay or offers to assist a transition.

They're going to miss me too, they will, they would if they tried, goodbye Rauan, seems right as well, meeting in this dumpy, well-known doughnut shop, your donkey baby won't fare well if you keep feeding him foreskins.

Hello, Page Looker, surprised I noticed you?

All these grunts and mumbles are for your benefit so pay attention.

Hello briefly, hello keep walking, hello to the lady in the black hat, hello with blank stare, hello to the people, hello to the guy I don't remember, hello fish bait, hello snake-skinned purse, hello and pretend, hello in a little kid's voice.

Hello Rauan.

Comparing my life on Facebook to Rauan's, watching it unfold through a stream, the daily parade of obituaries and plates of pretty food, the many legacies of meals, the memory of plate presentation outliving the memory of its heartiness or the memory of most humans.

Meeting at a restaurant with the word "sperm" in the name, taking a picture to post on my wall, somebody please like my picture, don't want to feel dumb for sharing, wonder if it was wrong to unfriend Rauan, commenting on terrifying vacation photos, automatically posting unread links, posting the good news about my weight loss, feeling dumb for sharing, I recognize the blue parrot face and consider accepting her friend request, smoothing over a misunderstanding on Facebook, Rauan changes his profile picture, refriending friends, fewer friends, I am dumb for sharing, blocking apps from my feed, don't fall for it, you can't track someone on Facebook, it's a trap, a lingering infection.

Facing Rauan to the rifle.

Bump on the face, red inflammation, painted strangely, the parrot girl's face fades into the stained glass, dry and cracking, a Magician's worn-off face, terrible bringing the ostrich to a fight.

Keeping a beat by hitting Rauan's face, hiding my face behind a flower bouquet, hideous beads sewn on my chin, buckshot, choosing our new faces after the cold-blood invasion and nothing fits.

Rauan brings a smiley face cookie.

I bring my shield.

We're bound to cookies and other things, a heart-shaped cookie broken in three, this war has to end, I'm going to align myself with Rauan.

We're gonna face her, together, we're not leaving until she gives us what we came for, she's going to answer to us, we will collect answers until the answer's weight locks us underwater.

We arrive to face her, Rauan with his vulnerable inflammation and I with my reflected sneer, we wait to face her, to face the face that turned her back.

Rauan walks the perimeter, I wait in the car, Rauan darns his socks passing time, I sleep in the car, Rauan licks his lips to detect the wind's direction, Rauan molds a trap from eggshells, Rauan screams all her names in an attempt to conjure her presence, hundreds, each one more vulgar than the last, I wake from my nap before I drown in piss and tears of exposure.

She never shows, doesn't even call.

A long, drawn-out letdown, a sick joke miming laughter, a crowning disappointment fit for a prince, Rauan broken into thousands, stewing, brewing like a scalding pot of singe, it's too much, I can't contain Rauan any longer, he's gonna blow or implode or barf or something.

Rauanrage and veins and marbled testicles.

Rauan leaves, runs up the hill intending to rape the Tree of Life for hours upon hours right in front of her helpless seedlings, forcing the seedlings to watch him meticulously hump each and every knot, forced to listen to him groan as he pulls acorns from his anus as he jizzes a steady supply of deep orange sap all over the tree's bark, I yell, *Think of the seedlings Rauan,* but Rauan doesn't think of the seedlings.

Does Rauan possess the ability to rape without corporeal form?

YES, THIS WILL BE A SPIRITUAL RAPE!

And I will be its accessory because I raised Rauan from unconception into misconception, Rauan goes back in time to teach primitive women how to hurt themselves, how to view other women as competitors, how there can only be one true daughter of the patriarchy.

Might that be dangerous?

I think that's the point.

Alone and terrified, I say something sort of like a prayer, a call for help and strength, not speaking aloud, but thinking, I think this is no place for Rauan, this is no place for anyone with tenderness in his heart for a mother.

Please don't let Rauan cross this boundary, even if it's just a failed attempt to cross. He'll be ruined. I'll be ruined. The tree aliens will poison us for being two of the hundred to change the world for the worse. I don't want anything to be worse. Please don't let us do any more damage.

I think *no more damage* over and over and over.

Then I'm no longer alone with my terror.

A Carry appears, practically a bag of splinters and dust, but she's here, grotesque in her mummified, lice-ridden, toothy way, but I'm grateful nonetheless for this ally because everything within is out of my hands.

So I put it all into her leathered palms.

Rauan, there's somebody here to see you, I yell up to him.

He thinks it's Mother, pulls up his pants as he trips down the hill, running like a child who needs to poop, he gets to me and looks around, "Where is she?"

I point to the wretched Carry knowing that's not who he meant, the Rauanrage thickens and I fear what he might do to me for this betrayal, fear thicker than a placenta served on top of a honeybaked ham, I turn to the Carry panicked, she speaks.

"In the beginning," she whispers into his ear, "we named you Rumpelstiltskin to banish you from our wombs, we had our reasons, reasons based on unwritten history and erased lineages, smolderings, reasons you'll never understand or accept, but today we grant you a place among us because you have suffered long enough to appease us. Today we rename you Rapunzel, you are new and corporeal, you are very real and a girl, you have long lush hair just like Axl Rose, you have a brain and a heart and all the courage that a pretty girl can muster going on her own to Grandmother's house, now go and be somebody, anybody, away with you, you belong to yourself and you are one of us, you can have it all which is absolutely nothing."

Rauan reanimates as a shape-shifting imp, Rauan as a female police officer whose job is to make me feel safe, but I don't feel safe, Rauan growing hands and toes, Rauan chasing the ostrich into the ladies room, Rauan stepping on eggs, Rauan in the virgin chamber, a seal, a mermaid, something with a flipper.

Rauan turns Rapunzel, uses her own hair as a lasso to swing away, laughing, "Me Rapunzel, you still nameless."

Text From Lily to Rapunzel (unconceived sibling formerly known as Rauan)

LilyInABox: ABCya, wouldn't want to be ya, Rumple Mintz!

Dear Diary,

A one-and-a-half-month old baby gave birth to a baby, knocked up in her mother's womb, born pregnant with impossibility, fetuses preying on fetuses, fetus on fetus crime, mother of all scandals.

    Oh the humanity of humanity.

    So much purchased from Babies R Us, the babies kept on having babies, Babies R TruckNutz, like multiplying twins, like a capitalist plague suckled by a bailed-out tit. Bailed out of an unspeakable heart that pumped black and purple, that pumped the rotten information, pumping air, pumping clogs into hairy ironies. Move along, there's no tangible milk here.

    All this tit's milk is only on paper.

    I went to the address on this tit's website but there was just a swamp.

    Nothing more than a pyramid tit scheme, a sagging one at that.

    This tit is gonna crash hard.

Visions of Bitches

Between a gauntlet of opposing dogs, she walked between two lines.

This was her path.

On one side, light brown coats, the other dark brown, each with markings of jigsaw puzzle pieces on their hindquarters. She was light brown, with dark spots. She could go either way but for now she moved straight and kept to the middle not wanting anyone to think she had an opinion or preference. The alphas would fight for the honor to be the one to mate with her for life. Most of the dogs weren't alphas and weren't in contention for any kind of mating but that didn't stop them from barking at her.

One of those not-alpha dogs wanted to mate with her for life very much. So much he turned to the moon howling his pleas. A woman appeared, perhaps his fairy godmother, told him how he could win the bitch's paw despite not being an alpha. She explained that the secret to a lifetime of mating with the bitch was to find the woman who kept a very special pillow underneath her bed and to take that special pillow from her while replacing it with a decoy. The not-alpha sniffed her crotch and went on his way.

When the not-alpha found this special pillow he discovered its special embroidered message: "Be careful what you smother." He knew he didn't have much time and needed to quickly replace the pillow and leave before the pillow's owner discovered him. But he couldn't not stop and hump that plump pillow and once he started he couldn't stop himself.

The Edwardian women watched from afar and discussed the not-alpha dog's situation amongst themselves.

From afar I watched the Edwardian women watch and discuss the not-alpha dog's situation. I turned to Lily and said: *This doesn't pass the Bechdel Test. There's the bitch, the fairy godmother and the woman with the fuckable magic message pillow, but they don't speak to one another and then there's a room full of women who do speak to one another, but choose to only discuss the mediocre man-dog.*

Lily nodded her head. I made a good point. I often make very good points.

She asked, "Yes, but do you have a name in this scene? Anywhere in the script? How will you appear in the credits? Will you ever be given credit? Do you even make receiving credit possible? Does your psychic memoir pass the Bechdel Test?"

Note from a Carry

This pose a motion, moving like an empty
retail space crammed with mannequins
asking, "Are we there yet?"

Your pose going out of business
hatching like spiders believing in the
benefits of crying a web to
snag relics of storge.

A forgotten baby existed.
The spiders spun and after
many years, they caught baby's head
lacking transparency.

What logic can be found in a baby's head?
An artifact with clues leading to its
missing body?

Solutions need to be posed.
Cheesecake and hot dog calendars to raise
money for a torso and chest are a possibility.

Adding a lawnmower pull to
restart the heart is another.

Break a heart-shaped cookie in
three and plant its pieces in the gravel.
Tell the lady wearing the webbed veil sitting
at the poker table that she wins.

Acknowledge that she looks
quite polished and graceful
like a granite Jackie O.

Convince her to relinquish her heart
for a diamond flush.
Give her the ice.
Jumpstart that baby.

Signed,
C

New Move

These days when I play chess, the obnoxious woman piece stands in for the prince. She's an obnoxious piece alright, flashing her crass tits at the first hint of weeping, but she's a muscular Olympian, so even though I don't understand and can't be bothered to learn how to pronounce her name, she's my piece in this game.

I can't claim to understand the game either. Like an algorithm, I stopped trying to understand it a long time ago.

Like a bacteria, I never had control of it.

Is it a good algorithm or a bad algorithm?

Is it a good bacteria or a bad bacteria?

Are those good fat tits or bad fat tits?

I stopped asking questions with difficult answers.

I just allow whatever needs to crawl inside and calculate its thing.

When I first played the game, I'd spend all my time filling in holes, but filling in the holes made things that I didn't want to happen start to happen. For instance, a naked man with very soft ass skin came over and said, "Please don't plug that hole, ma'am, you're going to need it later. Holes go both ways."

Studying the DNA of the obnoxious Olympian revealed that she had a more obnoxious twin: a circus performer with the audacity to improvise in the ring and expect the audience to chant her name as they cheered for more—which they always did. Every egocentric tweet she tweeted went viral. Every selfie liked to oblivion. She was both an acrobat and a singer, muscular and crass in an entirely different way.

I wondered, would it be possible to have two different women on the same side, on the same board, at the same time? Would the game stay the same? What kind of ruin might two women working together bring?

Would they have to rename it Princhess?
Lady Checkers?
Board Bitches?

Recovered Memory

Deer collapsed from disease all around the neighborhood; carcasses piled in the stairwells. The living weren't far behind. He asked if I cleaned out the corpses. I had not. Let someone else do the heavy lifting for once. I had a sinus infection.

Someone touched my face against my will. I already had plans. Surrounded by sock-monkeys closing in fast. A mother pushed a stroller next to a little boy holding a baby. I judged that woman and found her judgment to be guilty.

A mother should know how dangerous it is to surround children with monkeys. A mother should stand between her child and all unruly animals.

Deer season, our new death. A bald man behaved bizarrely in a Chalet of Lice and Dear and no one acknowledged it.

Really messaged up.

Letter from Lily

"When will my prince . . ." was never the scenario, yet your selections keep coming up princes.

The question is "when will my dodo . . .?" Do you remember that blue parrot-faced cat girl you dropped down the stairs? Might there be a retrospective reconstruction opportunity in the bowels of this grubby pit?

Truly,
Lily

Post Diary Entry Regarding an Archeological Status

The stranger improves but I'm still not returning him to his apartment. I'm not giving him his bath, not giving detailed instructions to someone else to handle this duty, not giving any explanation.

This is just not something I'm willing to nurture.

One time I walked into my house and found a well-constructed, naked stranger covered with scars and scratches soaking in my bathtub, felt like I should have recognized him but he said his name was Dread and back then I didn't know any Dread.

I didn't know how the knife or camera got into my hands either.

Not giving up my antidote or my anecdote.

Does the stranger continue to be stranger?

He's lingering too long over short passages, not giving necessary time for the longer.

How long will his lingering continue?

The best strangers linger until they expire, shroud themselves in dark clothing so their damage won't appear in selfies.

The best stranger is patient and forgiving with our fear, by never speaking of his own.

A muted, damaged muse who doesn't tell us when he hurts or ask our name makes the very best stranger.

Open Call for the Keeper of the Bird

The woman sitting on the bench wearing the black pointy hat, polished Jackie O bust, woman who lost her roof, wife who suffocated her husband with pumpkin pie, the black cat I tore to dirt, the snake skinner who mixes animal prints, the Blow Job Queen who reached a miserable fame, the witch-in-training waiting in the van down by the river, new age lady with the large and underutilized retail space, laundress in possession of the ancient Chinese secret, blonde Joan Crawford, Posh Spice in a hand-me-down, the hairnet who works in the school cafeteria, the Angelina Jolie-type going through some kind of change, Courtney Love from an old movie filmed with her original nose, the one who called me "sweet" while acknowledging she ate my waffle, the witch-doctor who doesn't understand technology, the drunken beast, Elvira, the collective mom-poets meeting in the tool shed, the crispy corpse, Clair Huxtable, the company woman sans pantsuit, the escaped dwarf, reluctant lesbian, Eminem's ex, Typhoid Mary, woman with a bad perm, drunk Diane Keaton, the confused hostess carrying a tray of cookies, penetration apologist, choo-choo train apologist, geisha with a bazooka, Leona Helmsley, the one vacationing in an institution, the chink in Sarah Palin's armor, the Avon lady, the moment when it happened, beard with the mullet, the enthusiastic dental hygienist, red dress, moonbeam, Mother Goose sans feathers, waitress with the wrong order, Sarah Connor, traffic cop stationed on Temporary Road, Martha Stewart, Mrs. Butterworth, Aunt Jemima, Jabba's slave girl, Baba Yaga baking bread, pregnant teenager wearing the Black Sabbath t-shirt, coked-up harpy, television star without her makeup, Anna Wintour wearing the latest lime-wedge couture, the crushed pizza box, ass-grabber at the Christmas party, whore talking on the pink RAZR, Andrea the Giant, patron wielding the steak knife, mummy full of lice, unsexed librarian, food stamp driving a Cadillac, Laura Palmer, Boy George, Athena's spite, Billy Jean's schemes and plans, the diseased willow, the flighty oak, the human spider, Gretchen Ross, everlasting roulette wheel, Glinda performed by Linda Tripp.

Which one of you witches is my mother?

Text from Lily

LilyInABox: 81tche$ 4nD h0e$,
81tche$ 4nD h0e$
d4t de$cr18e$ 4LL the w1mm1nz
1 n0e$!
L0FL!

Letter from the Carries

The contrast between the stylish mask and the functional smiley face and the women who loved the contrast.

The belief that computers could think like humans and the women who, at their own peril, questioned the intelligence of artificial parrots.

The fable parade carried over from last week's episode and the women who marched for the rights of witch practitioners.

The women who loved the bomb makers and the women who embraced mass destruction for all its brooding mystery.

The women who pursued strategy and the spiders who engineered their fishing shrouds.

When the women get all steamed up tell them their responses are manufactured imitations.

We are the monster-women who carried you back from the woods to the swamp's safety.

Intelligent behavior, like logic, is a fish story.

We are the snorkel-mask and here is our snout.

Signed,
The Carrier Collective

Recovered Memory, Found in a Diary

When I found the paths, I didn't really recognize them, glow-wormed, barely explored, bumpy with tree roots and snake skins, all trip and traipse and venom.

All paths lead to the attic of all places, to the dead-eyed, Medusa's Mausoleum, Decapitalist Museum, the hoarder's realm, where in the beginning I thought I wanted to be, but this is no escape, no detour, no fluffy pillow to bore into.

Mind flood: the dinosaur sex, septic tank inspector, country living, burning chapel, pearl broach, lifeboat fastened with band aids, magic carpet, crusader fashion, spider webs declaring orbs the new artifacts, candy corns, romance shopping, clowns without teeth, clowns with candy-corned teeth.

This is about selection.

What to forget so one can remember, editorial intent; the death of ownership, the death of flea markets, the rise of a lice economy.

Where's room for pleasure?

A room of no one's own, a shared room, crowded room, room with a pew, room with a trap door, room with schematics, hula hoops, menstrual streams, juvenile detention centers, piss, more piss, masks, splinters, snake scales, measuring scales, justice scales, scaling Mt. Market Value, scaling the Heritage Wall to find more room.

What do kids consider timeless these days?

Popularity, success, fame, those narrow urethra lickers and their conceptually bankrupt visions for an influential future.

What did the kids consider timeless back in the day?

Procedure, as normal instructions go, to press the start button, or blow, it's all being timed, orbular time-keeping, a game of pyramids and ruins, not too far off the map, too far off the orb, too far back when drawers had labels, etchings, cracked drawer holding a gray-liced mummy named Carry, holding a smaller drawer containing more carriers, the Carries, more nuisances, more vexations, every Carry an exception to a procedure, every Carry a crumbled institution, every Carry a monster and a mother and a machine and a muzzle, every Carry a carnival, dried carnation, carnotaurus, carnosine injection, carnot cycle, carcinogen, carnal knowledge, carnivore, a spectacular carnage.

Carry, singular of Carries, lone wolf McCarry, the carrier, as an informational-bearing signal, like a wave formed from the belly of misery, like a transporter of blackened flesh, the skin & scale train, as mutation who grows wiser over the course of something bigger than time, the carrier who can't get sick, like a charge free to move between and through lines, a ring-like algorithm wailing BOOlean because math stands the test of time, math lasts, math is real, the arithmetic idolaters and their impending punishment, ain't that the truth.

Unless it's false.

How silly to worry about faces when finding an ancestor like this.

Yet here's my need, so raw and fleshed.

The Things, I Try, I Carry.

Dear Diary,

Spider lugging a purse with a large shell, seashell really a turtle shell, taking the unwanted clam, clam on the deck, a conch and cross necklace, seashells shouldn't be perfect, oyster pearl on the screen throbbing, I pick the snake, I pick the wolf, I pick the dragon, I pick the spider, I pick the clam, I pick all the dogs and cats and other domestics, I pick at the inflammation and it just gets worse.

    Squeezing a clam from my palm until it pops worms. Once I painted dark things like spider webs, insect mummy surprise, newborn webbed faces, webs not catching the big pictures, cat-sized spiders, spiders riding rats, spiders mounting turtles in slow motion for the exposure.

    Back when exposure was all the rage.

    Three dimensional cobwebs can't bring down the cat, but they can bring down the reptile, rock, paper, scissors, cat, DRAGON, leopards hibernating in a snow pile, she's a leopard not a burden, she's a spiral not a pit, she's an overflowing spittoon, a molested mollusk hated for her success.

    The spider that spun her into an orb to quiet her.

    The spider who created the globe to contain her.

    A world where a man manhandles a dodo to get tenure,

a world where anything can be a crime or a hilariously inappropriate joke.

Do you know the one about the alligator and turtle racing in a pond?

The alligator spat on the window because he didn't like being observed swimming in circles. The turtle won because he lasted long enough to swim a second lap.

Like that 70's movie where the old man befriends a young child and a turtle.

It's called "The Turtle."

Turtle monuments, turtles acting as toilets for birds, the photo of the owl with the turtle, turtles from the black lagoon.

The flat leathery alligator revives itself, that movie where George Clooney takes the young woman to his beautiful, sophisticated bedroom, followed by the scene with the sloppy roommate ruining everything by bringing along that sock monkey.

Allegations about alligators, accusations about spiders and webbed intentions, am I sounding hardened to suffering because I'm thinking really expensive handbags and excruciating pumps.

An old-fashioned combination lock, voice over voice over multiple voices whispering from the lower drawer, looking through a drawer full of lice and fossils, finding miniature alligators with wings, alligator pillow biters, that episode where the Incredible Hulk playfully wrestles that alligator into a submarine, zombies climbing the towers hungry for Ph.Ds or maybe Cheetos, strolling down the lane, hand to an alligator's mouth, a discussion on the repercussions of attacking our boat leading to my smashing someone's head against a chest of drawers.

I'm coming to get you, you, you, food-chained being of misery, you feathered curse, you blue-faced child stapled on all my milk cartons.

Remedial Historical Introduction to Bombyonder

Bombyonder, the multi-layered frame accompanied by its partials and omissions sometimes intentionally visited for reflection and restoration, but often a psychic zone one wakes trapped inside, has always been popular with the tourists. A psychic tourist enters the Bombyonder to see the sights, take photographs, barter over pennies for souvenirs, mark spots off lists. A tourist is not interested in meeting herselves. A tourist enters without a moral purpose, unaware of the unconscious influences and forces. Tourists are often robbed and beaten. These assaults are always recorded and virally shared for the villains' posterity. Afterwards, dumped into gutters, ponds, casinos, mall food courts, tourists are left to die in merry irony.

Next you have your psychic thrill-seeker who wishes to wrestle with his soul not so he may glean or gather anything but for the rush, the high, the comical boner. Psychic thrill-seekers want a unique experience and impressive tale to recount at social gatherings. When tourists and thrill seekers venture into Bombyonder they're unprepared. When they get stuck, they're paralyzed, like a spider's prey unraveling like a hula hoop. They require retrieval before they're consumed and digested into arachnid shit.

If she's a true dingbat, either a psychic traveler or a poor hung-over soul who awakens to find herself in this zone, there's a more fortunate prognosis venturing through Bombyonder. A traveler makes her journey the top priority and, if she's alert, manages to recover a great deal during her time. A dingbat traveler plans ahead, but with enough flexibility to allow herself the freedom to investigate the unexpected and remain open to new alliances. Non-dingbat travelers often never leave the dock. They're too logical and foolish. Therefore they often don't realize they're in Bombyonder and therefore never leave.

In earlier times, when the metaphorical conceptions of ancient times were confused and misappropriated, people associated the Bombyonder with to "Hell," a physical, often fiery, place underneath the earth where people only went after they physically died. Some considered this a place set aside to punish sinners, diametrically opposed to an alternative sky realm, called "Heaven," for the non-sinning or sinner repentants. "Saving Their Seats in Bombyonder" was a successful congressional campaign slogan in 2020 that implied those who were against the candidate were already marked for an afterlife of unholy retribution.

Often 21st century medical doctors labeled Bombyonder as a symptom of a mental illness, like schizophrenia, or stress-induced delusion. One could understand how doctors reached these diagnoses considering that Bombyonder is rife with illness, both mental and physical, as well as a multitude of oddities and shams.

Other antiquated belief systems simply considered the Bombyonder more as the final destination for all after physical death, a place filled with spirits and gods, and less of a place of torment. Some believed one could reach Bombyonder only after a psychotic break.

What we know now is that the term Bombyonder describes a hole that leads to a personal section in the untold galactic necropolises that create themselves after a government or ruling system falls or irretrievably declines. The beneath-the-surface goings-on are like a family-run black market held in abandoned crypts filled with museums, libraries, schools, theaters, convenience stores, drawers, containers, wildlife, creatures, bodies of water, among other relics. Modern day psychic recording methods proved beyond doubt, that while one may never be privy to all the goings-on in Bombyonder, it is in fact quite real.

Much of the past confusion around the Bombyonder can be linked to what we call "linear thinking" and "reality versus fantasy." For several centuries (19th-23rd), the majority of societies considered it logical to construct a reality based on step-by-step thinking, evidence-based conclusions, timelines, etc. This primitive belief system was further supported by the concept that the "real" was limited to what we could see, hear, feel, taste, touch back when people knew of only 5 senses. As shocking as we may find this today, when we now know of at least 14 senses beginning with Medusa, it wasn't that long ago when something as basic and encompassing as "intuition" was dismissed as "archetypal feminine rage." Early education focused on teaching techniques that categorized information picked up by our senses into black and white divisions such as "true or false," "fact or myth" and "real or fantasy." Children and adults who dared challenge the finieval mindset were medicated, institutionalized, ostracized and beaten. We should not judge too harshly on those who followed the finieval beliefs. Following one's personal truth almost guaranteed one would be labeled as mentally ill or delusional. At best, one could pursue a growing awareness via artistic creation or a professional field such as psychotherapy, psychiatry, and scuba diving, and other professions where one could twist and conform truths into slightly misshapen boxes and call it science. In most cases, psychic awareness was a lonely and brutal life. We should not be so smug or sure that we would have conducted ourselves any differently than the cringe-inducing examples of our ancestors.

As we now take for granted, the Bombyonder is not a physical place that we can "touch" the same way we can touch our toes, we rightly recognize the much deeper touch. This unified greater awareness has increased our evolution at an unprecedented rate and offered humanity access to wisdom never before available. Some have embraced and honored this opportunity, while others have chosen to glean what is available but not wade too deep. Unfortunately some, as it has always been, are reckless. These psychic deadbeats put themselves in great danger for nothing more than cheap thrills and bragging rights. The bulk of my business (psychic retrieval) comes from rescuing these psychic deadbeats and mentoring them, by any means necessary, in the ways of psychic citizenship.

If they refuse, as some do, my job is to bomb them into reality, forcing them to begin the pilgrimage anew. No matter how many times it takes.

They have all the spirals of time they could ever need.

Letter from a Carry

The secret of the thumb drive.

    Secret of the sticky fluid.

    The subject matter divined from the muttering drunk, prolific and cryptic, fuzzy.

    The secret snapshot of the seductress, disease free, minimally hazed, sporting a fur-trimmed footsie.

    Like an investigation, you begin with a fake name and P.O. box.

    Like a quiz, it's 20 questions and 50 answers.

    Fact-finders read the texts without their 3-D glasses because they want to stay focused.

    The fact-finders don't mind if the world already came to an end as long as they have tangible proof to sustain the assertion that it's still spinning and they're still there.

Vague Recollections

The dead bird sang like nobody in a cage.

When I was the boycott, women stopped commanding canoes and sent the swamp to hell with their intentional spite.

When I was the refrigerator, the remaining fruit that hadn't yet deteriorated, exploded.

Believing was when worrying stopped and somebody wondered, "Now wouldn't that be wondrous?"

When I filmed commercials, I filled space and when I filled space, she'd fidget and scratch her face through the mask.

She could never tell the truth honestly, only with gravity and the weight of mistruths, which were her truths.

When I wrote my term paper I wrote about my spleen in order to learn what was possible without it.

What was gone could not be described or categorized.

When I learned what was possible, I deeply drowned and hoped not to be missed.

The sash crisscrossed a blank form into a fault.

Not mine, I insisted.

Recovered Memory

Late, my invitation rebuffed, but the cats were getting along so it could have been worse. Seemed a simple solution. I recalled all the men fitting into a single compartment. We played a four-piece game that wasn't particularly difficult for them to master and defeat me like someone designed the game to guarantee my loss. The difficulty came with the math equation afterward. I forgot how and couldn't relearn, no matter how much I tried.

My monsters grumbled in disbelief, mocked by both the media and peers for ever crawling into this drawer with me in the first place. Drawer full of navel-gazed oranges and lice. All the fashionable atrocities happening OUT THERE SOMEWHERE. Nobody cares about internal slaughter and abuse when there are robots snapping pictures of the holy battles on Lake Titan. Fucking robots, taking really significant photographs that would be gracing the cover of *Life*, if *Life* still existed.

But I, a grown-ass woman, insisted on my drawer, alternately cowering and raging over my mother. When I wasn't raging over my father or my husband or my pathetic lovers or my imaginary brother. I had 99 lady problems, but a robot wasn't one.

Or at least not one I recognized.

Give me a simple recipe, I pleaded. *Or a simple question or machine.*

I wondered if I had brain damage. It would be a relief to have brain damage. It would be nice to have an excuse, I thought.

I discussed the possibility of an excuse with my aunt and she offered one. There's an Italian descent in our family that makes the women get pregnant early and that's why we don't know math. I disagreed, I heard we were of Greek descent and those are two very different places to descend from despite often being confused by amateurs. Besides my aunt was often wrong. She didn't finish high school because she had a baby.

Eventually when I found our family tree, it was all Slovak and Celtic, not a Greek or Italian for centuries. We were raised making excuses to cover up that we were raised to search for mythical mates. Nobody ever said go to class or do your homework. They said, "You're the prettiest" or "You look like you're six months pregnant" before you ever had your first menstrual cycle just to shame you for finishing your fried dumplings.

So yeah, I embraced my true excuse.

Then the tremors came. Our tribe was disbanding. The women were taking their babies and settling elsewhere. We were expert settlers by genetics.

"This wasn't how it was supposed to happen," my grandmother said.

But this was how it happened and I laughed because she was old and the world grew into a scary place for her, but not for me. I was young and my flesh below my bicep hadn't yet swung. The ground opened and the Greco-Roman stairs presented themselves. Turned out we all were a little bit right about our origins.

We were to sink underground, find a myth and fuck him until we got something of our own to take away.

I couldn't recall whether I escaped from the tribe or if the tribe abandoned me, but same result either way. My fucking days were above ground and what I wanted in my belly was a bird.

Who was going to give me my bird?

Dear Diary,

Two spoons facing one another, spoons tied with ice cream, metal spoon, plastic spoon breaking, forks and spoons for cake, death by plastic spoons, small bowls and spoonful, fork gathering, a fork in the highway.
    Sandwiches waiting in the library.
    These kids are picky eaters, hot turkey, reasonable sandwiches, mixed-up sandwiches, she stole my cheese, drowns in gravy, slugs in the salad coming up invertebrate, sandwich not a sandwich omen.
    Salads again and again.
    Salad on the dinner plate, gummy worms and salad, bags of salad in a suitcase, salamanders eating fruit, comparing cookies to salary, salary salad with the entry-level pay grade, dressed in age-appropriateness.
    Bugs like short worms, pasta with worms, bloodworm like a flacid penis, worm-like armpit growth, worm-like creature at the root, brightly colored worms and their tentacle-like things raging for the tonsiled promised land.
    These worms taste like dick.
    Opting not to go the silly penis route.

Sperm cup, sea giant with a large penis growing from her chest, her penis tucked back, penis over pants, salty thin penis, getting some Neosporin for that penis, penis torment, stretch and pretend, the animal's penis, like a corkscrew, the animal's mouth, about to bite down on that penis.

I'm gonna watch.

Recovered Memory

Selecting the first two pennies to trade for admission was the easy part. The struggle was deciding on the final one. All the remaining pennies in my change purse seemed necessary. One was wheat, another steel, one covered in feathers, a strange one written in Hebrew and the rest were U.S. State collectibles. Which one would be the easiest to replace? Could I live without any of them?

The choice between the pinched and slighted. The choice to put on those rubber shoes and board the subterranean rocket ship. The choice between ordering oysters or swine for supper. Choosing my avatar's name and hair color.

A form with only two choices: Medieval Orthodox or Dingbatted Medusa.

Letter from a Mother

Sup, worm food. Heard about that dead bird. Heard you think that dead bird was a part of you. You wish something was about you. Nothing is about you. Every girl carries her mother's extinguished soul inside of her. Once a woman gives birth to a daughter a piece of her withers away. THAT'S what a daughter carries inside. You are a CARRIER.

    MY carrier.

    It goes both ways. And more. You carry everything that I wanted, but never got. You carry my disappointment. You carried it from your very first breath. When you barfed up that bird, you were repelling me, your own mother who gave up everything so you could live your dopey life, you ungrateful dingbat. That's why you're here, to try to reconnect with me. It's not about you, you dingbat, it's all about me and how you need me, yes you NEED me and that's tough shit for you because I'm not feeling particularly generous. What have you ever done for me?

    Time to plead, my darling. Time to make this all worth my while. I have no use for men or heretics in my monarchy. Repent your father. Repent your unconceived brother. Repent your slaughtered husband. Repent your horrific lover and your mangled, unshutable heart. Repent all your booty-called snakes and lizards. Repent your wolf in a box in a box. Never speak of them again.

    Now go make me a dodo pot pie, watch me devour it and remember I can do the same to you.

Signed,
THE QUEEN

Letter from Lily

How long are we gonna wallow here? Menopause is right around the corner and you're still worrying about what Mommy and Daddy think. Why didn't you bomb them for sending you here? Or smother them with a pillow for simply creating you for their vain assbeasted purposes? Worrying about ancestors and lineage. What about progeny? There's a dead little boy on a donkey and another little boy in need of a donkey. Where's our blue-headed step-daughter? Probably giving tug jobs behind a grocery store just to survive through your neglect. Sound familiar? Where do your responsibilities lie? There's a concept of priorities that you're blatantly neglecting while you lie here feeling sorry for yourself.

You're not supposed to be an assbeast. You're a dingbat. The whole point of connecting to your roots and memories is so you can recognize the dingbattery and with that newfound wisdom embrace the COSMIC DINGUS. If you want to get away from your mom, get your kids and crawl out of your father's hairy sphincter-crater.

I'm really starting to hate it here. Aren't you? We shouldn't put this off any longer.

Truly,
Lily

Recovered Memory

When I was a girl, I regularly wandered fields and open spaces. Sometimes there'd be men shucking husks and other times there'd be women's bodies strewn between the crops. I turned a blind eye to both the pie-making ventures and atrocities. Back then it was all the same to me, horrors to be rejected. Once I tripped and fell over half a six-pack. When I pushed myself up I observed a surfer ride the waves of corn. I thought, *ain't this America, ain't it?*

It sure was, I was pretty sure.

Texting with Lily

X: Did it ever occur to you that maybe you're stuck in a box inside a junk box because YOU'RE THE DINGBAT?

LilyInABox: I'm every dingbat.

X: WTFEver. They sent me to the Bombyonder to fetch my own damn bird and I don't know where to look.

LilyInABox: Are you going to take a name or what?

X: Call me Loop Donkey Bog.

LilyInABox: No.

X: Call me Rauanella.

LilyInABox: Ugh.

X: *Then call me Momsockella.*

LilyInABox: Maybe if you weren't so terrified of birth.

X: *Call me Princess Bombyonder of the Beyond Realm.*

LilyInABox: You're going to settle for the title of Princess?

X: Queen?

LilyInABox: You're going to name yourself after that wormy assbeast?

X: It would give me a socially acceptable motive to bomb her. I would replace her. Her power would be mine.

LilyInABox: Oh, is that how it works? You sound like your father. Very linear.

The Thing About Names

If I consist of a series of shattered mosaic shards and slivers that when put together form me in my entirety, this entirety being MYSELF, how would giving this thing a name help you to know me?

HELLO MY NAME IS _____

If the blank was filled in, would it be what you needed to know me? Aren't names merely symbolic pointers to the incomprehensible? Does it matter that the shards have been pulverized into dust and divvied up and moved and integrated with other objects, such as men and trees and swamps and a variety of animals and monsters? Does it matter that even if all the existing pieces could be put back together, the mosaic would never be the same mosaic that it was before? The entity that can never be the original entity.

What would the name tell you? Have you been reading all this time just to get a name?

HELLO MY NAME IS I FUCKED YOUR MOM LAST NIGHT AND OH BOY TALK ABOUT A SNATCH OF SNAKES I'M STILL SQUEEZING OUT VENOM FROM MY FIST.

I believe that above-named speck floating over the ass of an ostrich tells you far more about me than any name ever could and that's just a possible name of one microscopic sliver that could be extinct tomorrow.

What's the matter, too long for you? Would you prefer calling me Snatch of Snakes for short?

You don't get my name because my name doesn't get me. What I'm saying is my name isn't my name. Your name isn't your name either, but keep telling yourself that it suits you.

And tell your mom I'll be over again tonight with a fresh bag of mice.

Text from Lily

LilyInABox: OMG. What. Was. That?
I think I just detected a queef in the force. That definitely was a hissy queef.

The Thing About the Future

There can be no future without an inheritance. You can't make something out of nothing. If you think you did, you're kidding yourself. You built this using something already built by another. Oh the passionate assholitude of the delusional independent-minded!

Nothing times nothing equals nothing, no matter how many parentheses you put around it. You need to reappropriate something to stick into that algorithm.

(Medusa + dingbat) x (wolf + cat) / (worms – ostrich) x (donkey / dragon) – spiders = Carry

Dig it.
Swallow.

Recovered Memory

While I stayed back ensuring that the unrepresented received their tax receipts from the cashier, Medusa sliced like the greatest thing through the wicked with her patriotic shield.

Where was she all the times I fought the gelatinous tooth monster? I wondered.

All this time I used my shield as a mirror to redirect gazes, I never thought to use it for the offensive. Never thought to fight tooth and Jell-O with circular razor-sharp metal. Never thought something not shaped like a penis could be so penetrating and invasive or that the gelatinous monster would keep bouncing back. I never thought the Queen could be cut down, such a massive blob of dentata.

The Time of the Queen has Come

If there was such a thing as time in the Bombyonder, it was the time that I came for the Queen. Dressed in scabbed red flesh fitted to accentuate her blobbed silhouette, with bloodworms for hair, she was pure monster, the very monster I envisioned from the start. Exactly as recorded and remembered.

A distinct monster specifically created to torment me. But I prepared. I brought along my shield and my pillow.

I've come to smother you.

"You've come to mother me?" She smiled, a worm wiggled out from her nostril.

No, SMOTHER you with this embroidered pillow. I've come to kill you. I'm going to place this pillow over your face and hold it down. You're going to stop breathing. When that happens I will feel like a sack of feathers. My breathing will immediately improve. Then I'm going to slice off your head with the edge of this shield. I'll be so happy, I'll likely dance a jig on your belly. This is your end. Don't embarrass yourself by begging for my mercy. You won't get it.

"Oh too bad, it would have been nice to have been mothered."

Yes, it would have been nice to be mothered. But I didn't know anything about mothering any mothers or mothering anything at all. Even if I did, I wasn't about to mother my own damn mother. I sensed a cruel cycle, a familial pattern passed on for generations. I was confused. If she was a monster, which I certainly believed, then killing her would make me the hero. But if she was just my mother, well, that would make me the monster and I didn't want to be a monster like her. Maybe I was already a monster which would be OK as long as I was a different monster. Maybe we were the same monster? Maybe I was talking to my reflection in a shield and my reflection was responding in a Worm Queen mask? If I killed my reflection, would I die? Was I about to commit unintentional suicide? Like a dingbat?

I stood there, not moving, looking at her looking like a wormy blob, wondering how did I come from something so foul? Was I that foul too? Should I turn the shield toward my own face and observe my reflection?

"I hear you've been hanging out with some Carries. Did they teach you the secret of telekinesis? Maybe you can trap me in a closet and kill me by meditating on your numerous intentions."

Mother kept smiling, not that she seemed happy. Her smile seemed more like a mask. A mask covering I don't know what, but it frightened me. Like behind that smile could maybe be a semi-mighty kong with rabies.

I tried not to look frightened. I made fierce faces, breathed Ujjayi hoping she would mistake me for a dragon or whale.

"Are you going to get on with your matricide or what?"

I wasn't sure what I was confronting. After all this time, I was less sure of myself than when I entered Bombyonder. Should I risk killing what I didn't understand? If I didn't know what she was, how could I anticipate the consequences? She repulsed me, for sure. What if she sprouted more heads or worms? What if her corpse reanimated? What if some scientist appropriated her corpse and received all the credit?

I changed my mind, I'm not going to kill you like some common dude would kill his dad. I don't want to take your place. I don't want to sit on your throne or mount your horses or wear your wormy wigs. What I want is the blue-faced parrot cat. Give her to me and you may live, alone, among your worms.

"I never had her. Never even got close."

But you wrote she was your extinguished soul? I have your letter right here.

"That's right—everything I wanted, but never got, given to useless you."

I thought you were the Queen of Bombyonder?

That's what my father always told me. All my anger and mood swings, fits of tears and lethargy came from her. Irrational like Mother, needy like Mother, hysterical like Mother, deranged like Mother, petty like Mother, limited like Mother, the numerous shortcomings of Mother, the massive letdown of Mother. Source of it all.

"I'm Queen of being the Queen. A state of mind, really. You're an adult. I have as much control and influence as you allow and, by the way, you've been a real cunt about that lately. Smug as a butt plug, like your father."

Was the queen a liar? She seemed quite earnest. Like my father? I wasn't like either of those assbeasts. I wasn't. Was she mocking me? There was no smile on her blobular. Despite my algorithm, despite my orb and pencil, despite my Lily in the box, my shield, my shoes, my flowing hair, my confusion grew more profound than ever.

  Mother continued, "Do you know what your father promised me when we met? A better life! He said he'd pluck me from my godless slum and provide things for me, a better standard of living. I thought he meant opportunities. That I'd be able to do things. I thought I could go to art school or travel. He meant designer clothing and better hairdressers. He meant boring parties where after dinner the men went into one room to talk about worthwhile topics while the women went into another to talk past boyfriends. There is nothing worthwhile about boyfriends. The world I thought he was offering wasn't the world he was willing to give. He found me wild and exotic and in need of some polishing and civilizing. Basically what he offered was a Pretty Woman makeover on an academic's budget. He tried to force me to fit into his world, tried real hard with the help of lots of therapists and pills. He wanted to get me right so I could appear worldly and enlightened and impress those who lived in his world. A pill to curb your cursing. A pill to straighten your hair. A pill to improve your aesthetic taste. A pill to make you less confrontational. A pill to make you more approachable. A pill to make you less threatening. A pill to make you likeable. A pill to make you not care. Oh your Daddy loves prescribing them pills. He's real good at that. Not real good at much else though."

  My big moment, the part in this narrative where I face what I've been avoiding all this time was as fruitless as my avoidance. Stuck enduring tales of how I ruined her life, how he ruined her life, how they ruined her life, her fabulous, full-of-potential life if only, if only it wasn't for all of us.

  I don't care about that nonsense. I had nothing to do with what happened between you both. I'm the victim of both of your assholitude. What I care about is finding the bird. I need to swallow her or give birth to her or do something to make her mine, make all of this stop.

I still had no idea what I was supposed to do with the cat-faced blue parrot. After all this time, I didn't even know what she was or what she could do or what she was for.

"You should care. I am your mother. I gave birth to you. I didn't have to do that. I didn't have to throw it all away for a pathetic whiner."

Yet you did. So who's pathetic now?

"YOU ARE PATHETIC."

Her worms turned blood red and began to furiously wiggle and convulse. It dawned on me that I wasn't going to get what I needed following this line. She wasn't going to help me as long as I kept fighting her. I had to give her something to get something.

Fine, I am pathetic. I am a terrible, selfish daughter who was never worthy of you. In a blood pact with my father, we ruined your life for our own entertainment and pleasure. We conspired against you because you were so much better than us. We resented your beauty and promise. It's all terrible people can do. Destroy what's truly worthwhile.

"Do you really mean that?"

Absolutely. Isn't it obvious? Look at me.

She smiled. "How do you plan to make amends?"

I already have. I murdered father and I appear before you as I am, a life and soul in tatters, the karma from our evil played out. I am completely ruined.

"Why did you kill your father?"

Because he was a dick and really ugly. Old, a total has-been. He had it coming, didn't he?

"He certainly did. Tell me about your father's death. Details. I want details."

I cut his throat . . . but first I tied him to a chair in his laboratory and invited hobos off the street to bukkake him. I wanted him to feel shame. That went on for hours. I uploaded the photographs that I took and put them on Facebook. I tagged him in the photographs and made them public so all his colleagues would see. Then I showed him what I did. He begged for his reputation. Like a bitch.

"What did he do when he was splashed on?"

Oh he cried, begged me to untie him, told me he'd do whatever I wanted if I would just make the jizz stop. But naturally I ignored him. I told him his new name was Professor Jizz Cup. I changed his name to that on Facebook too. I never saw him so upset!

"I'm enjoying this narrative. Go on."

Well, after I ran out of hobos it was getting kind of late and I wanted wrap it up. There was a live Reddit chat I wanted to participate in. So I took a knife, a real dull, rusty one that he used to open letters and jammed it in his throat, which was saggy, like a turkey gizzard covered in liver spots. Father did not age well. He lost all his hair and his nose and ears got real big, sprouting hair and lord knows what else. He was plenty hideous before the jizz and death by neck slit. Frankly, he should have thanked me for killing him.

"When you cut his neck, what came out?"

A couple lame mules, a buzzard and some green oatmeal-looking stuff. Nothing of consequence.

"I knew it! How I wish I could have been there!"

Yeah, you would have really enjoyed yourself. When I get back home I'll send you the video.

"Thank you. I would appreciate that."

Of course. As soon as I get out of here.

"Dingbat. You can leave whenever you want. You already swallowed your blue cat-bird when you almost drowned in the swamp way back when you first got here. Gulped her like a guppy. You birthed her years ago, she crowned like a pearl emerging from a clam all while you dreamed in your sleep. The bomb was just a way to cut her loose, to find her in the rubble, get a glimpse so you'd recognize her. So you'd know she existed."

Then why am I still here?

"Because, you dingbat, you haven't clicked your heels yet. You gotta click your heels or wish on a death star or drink my blood or commit some kind of ritual. How I birthed a dingbat like you, I'll never understand. I had my whole life ruined. I could have went to prom. I could have worn a rose corsage."

Why are you so hateful?

"Because that's how you and your father chose to record me. I'm not sure which is worse, being twisted into the memory as a monster or being erased from history."

Don't blame us for how we remember you. We remembered what you left us. What you did to Rauan was cruel. You are a true monster.

"Oh boo-hoo, the ruined future of such a promising young man. He could have been a contender or a college athlete!"

He loved you. You withheld all love and acknowledgement from him. He deserved better.

"We're talking about the tree rapist, right? For fuck's sake, who doesn't deserve better? You think I deserve a life of worms? Of course you do. You are the most pathetic feminist I ever met. Picking a rapist over your own mother. After everything I sacrificed. Sickening."

She paused for a moment, wiped the worm that had been hanging from her nostril during the entire conversation and held it in her hand, looking at it, stroking it. I don't want to go overboard here, but she might have experienced a moment of self-reflection. And as cruel as she'd been, even at that moment, she was being helpful. Her responses did not feel like riddles or distraction. She did not confuse me. I gave her something that she wanted and returned the favor. A successful transaction.

Our most successful.

"If it bothers you so much, make it so I did something you'd find more palatable," she said as she flicked the worm into my eye.

Text from Lily

LilyInABox: Come on, is that really how it went down? I heard she gobbled you up and shat you into sausage links for her worms to feast on. That's what I heard.

Dear Diary,

Without an imaginary world, without a proper backpack, without my little pink orb, without an old tablet's commandments, without a hair dryer, empty hands, empty birdcage obscured by a crate of empties.

 Left without a predictable choice, without direct involvement, without being wiser, left without leave, left what I came with, left with myself.

 Squawkless, peepless, no doubt brandless.

 Nothing happening, nothing I wanted, nothing needed, nothing harmed any more than it already had been, nothing like a vacation to the bottom and getting fogburned.

 Discriminatory questions as I pass through the hole, am I this or am I that, would I say this or would I say that, if I could be any monster, which one would I be?

 There could have been a lollipop garden for me on the other side or a newly shined guillotine.

 I could have an army of bridesmaids wielding shields of bananas, enjoying my pillage.

 If you pencil them in, they will come.

 In some unpleasant, uncalculated fashion.

Dear Diary,

Finally found a cabinet with a Carry completely redone and in need of repainting, a glass cabinet with a lot of old knickknacks and books, a cabinet designed to hold crafts, like a filing cabinet but wider, the cabinet where the drinking glasses went, right next to a closet, full of lice, packed in containers with puppy veneers.

I discovered that once there was a national mothering cabin, a cabin open for people to eat their produce while not worrying about worms.

But it burnt down years ago.

After the fire, work began on a large replica, similar to the cabin where Lincoln once slept. Then some pasty motherfucker came by and chopped down all the trees and lied about it so they put him in a position of extreme authority and now he calls the shots and can no longer tell a lie because the framework becomes the truth.

Find me another cabin, one that is willing to serve a few good women, a cabin built as a triangle with a permit, a cabin with a Jacuzzi, gourmet kitchen appliances, super furry window treatments, a cabin designed to collapse when its usefulness ends.

Afraid to share as much as I have, details to share with a man, it really sucks to share such a small space, willing to share the bathtub, share the pie, share with my boyfriend, share my criticism, rather not have someone share my bed, we share the tacos, toothbrushes, an intimacy of plaque that partners share, there's enough to share, but let's keep something for ourselves. Sharing my fish, sharing my snakes, my orbs, pencils. Will I remember this? Will I be remembered as having a value? Will I remember what I gave and what I was given? What will I select and what will be selected for me? To be remembered is to lose control of yourself.

What does it mean to be remembered and do I desire such a thing?

I do not. I want to be seen while I'm here and when I'm gone, I'll have moved on and won't think of this place any longer and wish the same in return.

The relationship between the man and woman sharing a tomb, I mean really sharing it with the plan of sharing, sharing a single, sharing the same seat on the school bus, it wasn't about her sharing her attention, it wasn't about the lack of food, lack of care, instruction, fondness. It wasn't about everything I lacked.

But it was.

I am not a great man and I will endure no tests of time.

I am no great woman, I am not capable of lending any kind of stabilizing or support.

I am nobody's daughter.

I am a Carrier weighed down by afterthought.

Farewell to Animals & Miscellany

A dog bites my wrist. A tiger bites my hand. A zombie bites my arm. From the bush a snake bites my shoulder. The dragon cauterizes my bites. The clown vampire says, "I vant you to suck my dick," like he's straight up Transylvanian.

I'm just trying to get to the bakery to buy some edible muffins and get out of here.

The bird is pissed and tries to peck out my teeth before I get a chance to bite anything back.

I toss a lemon in the brush, tell them to suck it.

I toss my shoes and they all go fetch.

They all seem to fly towards my shoes.

They all make it impossible to make the point that money needs to be made here.

We all make choices for another's extinction and category.

Can't we all get along?

I don't think so.

We all need to eat.

Inevitable, Long Overdue Reunion with the Blue Parrot-Faced Cat Girl

The sasquatch who captured my heart met with me for a date at a popular chain funeral parlor. I didn't recognize him because he shaved it all. Every bit. Living as a sasquatch when you're so good looking is a crime against humanity, I thought. A positive change that will no doubt attract many admiring ladies. Just thinking about it made me ache with jealousy.

I told him, *I loved you against all odds and algorithms.* Which was totally true, when life was already harder than it needed to be. When it could have been simple, it became even more wretched with my love toward some repellant version of him, in some vile incantation, some twisted variation. No peace I wouldn't destroy my for love of a man, even if I didn't much like him.

At the funeral to put all this to rest, I noticed a young man with buck teeth in the elevator reflection. He wore yoga clothes while everyone else dressed in formal attire, mostly dark dresses with outrageous feathers. This was supposed to be the young man's funeral so I told him that it was especially important to be dressed appropriately. He agreed and wanted to change, but was afraid to go past the elevator where all the frightening faces pushed through his reflection to meet up with a never ending series of masks.

You just have to wade through it and try not to wretch in the stench of face rot. It only gets worse with time. It's always easier now than later.

A lovely service beyond the reflection. Endings are always lovely when there's flowers, plump-cushioned chairs and chocolates. Up front a pine box with a well-dressed sleeping boy. Some lost mother wept quietly in a corner. Good, she finally saw him and came to her senses, I thought. Sweet boys aren't supposed to survive for very long. Not here, at least. He's so much better off not here.

At the podium stood a young woman with remarkable blue poise and a decent amount of feline grace speaking a sermon, of sorts:

"I summon help from the yonder with this confluence software to allow us to pursue something a little more ambitious for ourselves.

"I summon the husbands and wives, brothers and sisters, and all those who aren't allowed to speak aloud, who secretly communicate with one another through tubes, I summon you to write in your diaries of acid-free pages and self-publish. Or not. Record the unrecordable and never apologize for doing so. You are not wrong to love or ache. You are not wrong to rage. You are not wrong to recognize the wrong. You are not wrong to name the wrong.

"I summon the oppressive and strange for remedies and possible treatment plans. Don't be the Ken doll talking science. Be the inflatable woman who gives tours of the whale's underbelly. Utilize all your holes; there's more than you know, more than could ever be filled over the course of centuries. Keep your boundaries strict and taut like police officers and when the time is right, everything topples appropriately. Do not be afraid of destruction. It's your finest tool.

"I summon a round button to respond to the past, this one and the next and all the rest that are to come.

"I summon a large retail space to be managed by a witch-lady and implore you to make good use of this space. Are we good witches or bad witches? Can we not be both? Yes, we shall be both! The terrible can be wonderful. Be wonderful souls with the most terrible desires. Let us ache in our own repulsiveness and never try to dull that ache.

"I summon the alienating doubt that more people will arrive in the form of love between citations, along with all the disadvantages of boredom, with lack of tragedy and the capability to interpret the wrong as a film about love through bedroom fog. How terribly love will do you when you understand and even more so when you do not. Ladies and gentlemen, there's a lot of love in these footnotes and it's all festering. Go ahead and squeeze it. I call on all of you to sing love songs over a cell phone as a daily response to love and its rot. Never make it think you forgot.

"Fuschia rhymes with Medusa and it is positively glorious. Slip on your fuschia negligee. Work it in and sing it, my people, you are what you remember and what you allow to pour forth from your mouths and fingers no matter what you make public and what you choose to keep to yourselves.

"Never worry for a dead bird. Never worry for anything fortunate enough to break free."

The Myth Reconstructed

Once upon a time my sister and I were born to our parents: a zookeeper and his former circus-performer wife, the world renown Bertha Schmitt. While she performed numerous acts, she was best known for gobbling up an entire swamp house, including the cement, glass, wood and asbestos. The video montage of her feat was viewed over a million times on YouTube. People called her the Queen of Eat. She could digest anything while smiling with delight. How did she do it they wondered? Of course there was a trick. She received a great deal of help from the countless worms in her belly.

Our parents named my sister Rapunzel which she liked very much and because she liked her name so very much, she was Mother's favorite. Every night Mother read Rapunzel cautionary tales while brushing her long golden-orange hair as they laid in bed together, high up in a tower far away from all the creepy boys and their gross penises. Father didn't mind that they spent so much time together high up in their tower, because he owned a great deal of barnyard creatures that needed his constant attention else they would cannibalize one another and take over the place. He spent his days building and mending fences for order. The community appreciated his careful caretaking of the property and increasing value. Over time this appreciation morphed into respect.

My parents gave me a name too, but I refused to remember it. I didn't like my given name and didn't like Mother and she didn't like me, so early on I said *Stay out of my way* and she said, "Fine by me."

And everyone was totally cool with that.

When I came of age, I announced to my father that I was striking it out on my own. My intentions were to research and search out thousands of Carries until I found one or more worthy to carry on. As much as I might have wanted, I couldn't make something out of nothing. I needed templates and materials. I needed roots and a base to start with. Father offered to make some calls on my behalf, put in good words, allow me to bank the influence of his name.

I said, *No thank you.*

"The world is a terrible place for a woman to be alone, without support and protection. Always has been and always will be."

So is the home.

He didn't acknowledge that, but asked if I needed some money to help in my journey.

I said, *No, but I would like to take the blue bird with me.*

He scratched his head and looked around—"You mean the blue pussy cat?"

Whatever you want to call her, just put her in this box and I'll be on my way.

"I don't see what good a cat will do you out in the world," Father shrugged, took the blue being and dropped her in my box. "Did you see Rapunzel's new rose tattoo on her ankle? Your mother went into quite the tizzy when she saw it. Couldn't tell if she didn't approve of tattoos in general or simply jealous because she never got her own. Maybe on your way out you might like to stop by and see it. Perhaps say goodbye to them in person."

Rose tattoos are common and vulgar and I'm in a rush.

"Very well, would you like to slit my throat before you go?"

Nah, I'm good. Besides if I did that I'd have to stick around and take over caring for your menagerie. Leave the inheritance to Rapunzel. I prefer to strike out on my own.

"You do realize it's going to be utter chaos until you develop some kind of workable structure. At the rate you're going, that could take a very long time, if it ever happens at all. You've never been much of an engineer and your creations tend not to care much for you, let alone survive. You lack a mother's touch among your other significant shortcomings."

But your father's touch makes up for it all, doesn't it?

"I'm just saying there's already structure and a good way of life right here. There's no need to go off subverting a perfectly-working hierarchy with you rampant uncertainty. You can mold a usable self right here without ever leaving."

It's not the self I want.

Father nodded, muttered, "My legacy hurts me more than it hurts you. But go on, claim your autonomy. You'll see it's not so easy. You'll see why I made the decisions I did. You'll see that all the suffering and cruelty were necessary and for the greater good. You'll see and more importantly, you'll be back."

Then he turned his back, returning to his cultivation of animals and cages.

As I walked away I tried my best not to look back, not to take one last gaze at the house, the farm, the fields, the animals or the tower and its occupants. Show him that not only was I not coming back, I wouldn't be thinking back in his direction, his version.

I really tried.

Not long after I departed with my blue being in a box, I approached Bombyonder's limits that opened into a crossroads of sorts. Hundreds of signs pointed to a variety of yonders, clearings, habitats, nooks, reservations and accommodations. Like a box of glowing orbs, you never know what might ruin you next.

As I contemplated my next move, I heard something behind me. I turned and saw a young man riding on a donkey. Yes he was quite fetching and I wondered what kind of partner he would be. I wondered if he had strong and straight teeth. I wondered the kinds of things I knew weren't helpful to wonder, but if you think there's a cure for such wonder or if you think there's some kind of lesson I should have learned by now, well you don't understand the mechanics of the human heart. Luckily none of us last forever.

As he got closer I recognized him from a long time ago.

Familiar and all grown up.

Hail, Oedipus. What big muscles you have now!

And what blood-shot eyes he had too.

Acknowledgements & Notes

Grateful acknowledgement is made to the editors and publishers of the following publications in which parts of this book first appears: *American Poetry Review, Beltway Poetry Quarterly, BOOG City 8, The Chapbook #3, Devouring the Green, Drunken Boat, Eleven Eleven, Fringe, Hobart, HTMLGIANT, Map Literary, MiPOesias, PEEP/SHOW, Redux, The Rumpus* and *Similar Peaks*.

Page 123: "All roads diverge from Medusa's head" is from Bruce Covey's poem, "The Difference Between Segments and Vectors."

Page 227: "Unarmored as I am   you can / take my head for your fucking / chaste warrior shield" is from Hoa Nguyen's "Medusa Poem."

Heartfelt thanks to the following people who gave their support and help with this book: Rauan Klassnik (my creeping psychic muse), PF Potvin, Brent Terry, Laura Carter and of course my dear publisher, Bruce Covey.

Love and everlasting gratitude to Chris & Gideon Morrow, whose love and support give me the space to write.

About the Author

Reb Livingston (www.reblivingston.net) lives in Northern Virginia with her husband and son. She curates the Bibliomancy Oracle (bibliomancyoracle.tumblr.com/askoracle).

Other titles by Reb Livingston:

The Fallacy Carriers of Bombyonder (The Chapbook #3, 2014)

God Damsel (No Tell Books, 2010)

Your Ten Favorite Words (Coconut Books, 2007)

The Bedside Guide to No Tell Books - Second Floor, ed (No Tell Books, 2007)

The Bedside Guide to No Tell Books, ed (No Tell Books, 2006)

Other titles by Bitter Cherry Books:

Reveal: All Shapes & Sizes by Bruce Covey